IN COLD PURSUIT

IN
COLD
PURSUIT

A NOVEL OF SUSPENSE

by Ursula Curtiss

DODD, MEAD & COMPANY · New York

1 2 3 4 5 6 7 8 9 10

Library of Congress Cataloging in Publication Data

Curtiss, Ursula Reilly.
  In cold pursuit.

  I. Title.
PZ3.C94875In [PS3503.U915]   813'.5'4   77–22447
ISBN 0–396–07466–9

F
CURT
c - 1

1

She had named the stray cat Dietrich when she adopted him—one of the few things she had ever done over her husband's objections—because of his long and shapely legs with their beautiful markings.

He did not look like an instrument of disaster, except possibly his own. He had none of the brooding mystery or even the coordination of other cats. He bumped into the furniture occasionally, recoiling in terror at his own clumsiness, and got readily marooned in trees although he was no longer a kitten. Dripping water fascinated him: he could often be found sitting in the sink, staring hopefully at the faucet. At times it seemed conceivable that he was another kind of creature entirely, dressed up, for purposes of acquiring a home, in a four-legged suit of tiger-striped fur.

But a gentle creature, not a decoy.

When he was not back from one of his undoubtedly

problem-ridden patrols by after seven o'clock on that May evening, his mistress finished a row of knitting, put down the mass of yellow wool, and went to the door to call him. This was the one night a week when her husband worked late, and although he tolerated Dietrich he was not fond of having his long-awaited cocktail and dinner to the accompaniment of frequent cat-summonings. Moreover, the weather forecast said rain, and in this as in so many other respects Dietrich was lacking; he would not discover what was going on until he was soaked and shivering. It followed as the night the day that he was prone to bronchitis.

"Dietrich?" The outside light showed her briefly before she moved out of its circle on her way to becoming a statistic: a tallish woman in her early thirties, slender in jeans and shirt, with cropped dark hair lying in points around an amiable, open-featured face. "Dietrich?"

There was nothing to indicate another presence in the tree-lined driveway, nothing to suggest that the house had been watched last week and the week before—in fact, since shortly after they moved in— and an increasingly interested note made that on this particular evening the carport stayed empty much later than usual. And that there was a woman alone here.

"Diet—"

The hand clapping over her mouth from behind almost stopped her heart as well as her breath. She knew what this was even before the tightening of the wiry arm across her chest and the warning as to the consequences of screaming. She wrenched her head

2

around and screamed anyway, into the light rustle of wind and the sound-absorbing trees, because noise was supposed to be the best deterrent.

It was an interrupted scream, because he hit her hard and she went sprawling backwards, her head driving against something sharp. For a few seconds the astonishing pain took up all her consciousness, and then she was aware of a pointed face close to hers —he had followed her down like a flash—and his rough, single-intentioned hands.

The familiar admonitions crackled through her brain like sparks of light. *Every woman's handbag contains an impromptu weapon.* She had no handbag. *Stamp on the assailant's instep with a high heel, or kick sharply backward at the shins.* She was wearing Indian moccasins, and she was in no position to kick. She got her wounded head up, seized one of the hands, bit down on the thumb as hard as she could.

Instantly, furiously, a knife appeared, calling to itself a dull dangerous shine even in the obscurity under the trees, but in order to get at it he had had to shift fractionally and she rolled away, caught at bark, staggered upright. Now she could kick, something warning her as she did so that she could not really hurt him but only enrage him further.

The warning was accurate. In the space between one second and the next she was fighting not against being raped but against being killed. She was strong and her reflexes were fast, but she was powerless against a knife, and in her terrified recognition that this was happening and could have only one outcome no matter how she fought, she felt the homing point of the blade in her chest scarcely more than the flash-

3

ing stings around her head and face.

Into a world limited to the sound of their breathing, hers straining through sobs, his savage, shot a new sound, rocketing, two-noted. An emergency vehicle. Unlikely as it seemed, someone had heard her cut-off scream and called the police.

It froze the boy—somehow her senses defined him as that—for the seconds that counted. She ran for the end of the driveway, or thought in her stumbling process that she ran, and only realized when she reached it that the police car or ambulance or whatever it was had shot by the mouth of the street and had nothing to do with her at all.

She looked wildly over her shoulder. The front door of the house was closed—had the wind blown it shut? Had she left it on the latch? Was he in there, waiting for her to come back and telephone for help? She couldn't think clearly; she couldn't even see clearly. She raced a bent wrist across one eye and then the other, and it came away sticky. Then, knowing that he was not in front of her, she began her effort at running again.

2

Automatically, because she had grown up among people so optimistic that they expected to win national contests and thought the police would forget all about that parking ticket, Mary Vaughan felt a little jump of alarm at the keening warble that began to swell in the night when she was a mile from home.

She reassured herself at once, a process she had to go through so often that the proper arguments unfolded neatly in her mind. Jenny didn't smoke, so it could scarcely be fire, and heart attacks or other seizures were rare among eighteen-year-olds.

There had been an armed robbery in the neighborhood a month ago, when a nice-looking couple pleading a need for a telephone because they had just passed an inert body by the roadside had suddenly produced a gun, tied up the elderly woman who had let them in, and gone methodically through her house. Mary had told her cousin about that, pointedly, because Jenny seemed to feel that after New York, Santa Fe was a harmless backwater.

The warble was on top of her now, along with flashing lights, and it was a coronary unit, hospital-bound. Still, Mary could have sworn at herself for forgetting, once more, that she could not reach her house by the usual route; a whole stretch of road was being disembowelled. She found a shoulder wide enough for turning, drove a half-mile back, was momentarily confused at a crossroads which looked different at night in a beginning rain, was finally home.

"Jenny?" She needn't have bothered to call reassuringly as she used her key; the living room was shadowy and untenanted, and the shower rushed obliviously. An odd scent wafting from behind the bathroom door suggested that her cousin had been doing something exotic in the way of face-creaming first.

In her bedroom, Mary changed out of her dinner clothes and into a housecoat. She had already decided against—the point of the dinner—throwing in her lot with the art director who had left the advertising agency at the same time as she, in the course of a reorganization, and the man who would be putting up most of the money for a new agency. She knew Al Trecino only by rumor and reputation; in the flesh, cold and larcenous under the easy-going charm he wore like the fisherman's sweater which was his trademark, he gave her the shivers.

Jenny stayed in the shower. Mary dismissed a few thoughts about her water bill, and in the kitchen— she felt like a hospital dietician—inspected the quiche lorraine she had made for her cousin's dinner.

A very small wedge had been cut out and the rest sealed neatly under foil. The lettuce left washed and ready had evidently been consumed, but not, according to the testimony of a squeezed half-lemon, with salad dressing.

Mary reminded herself to take this philosophically and returned to the living room, furnished in stone-blue and rose-brown against its white walls, and switched on more lamps. Somewhere during the past few minutes she had recorded the sound of another siren—had the warning flares on that disrupted section of road been extinguished by the rain, and an unwary motorist plunged in?—but she had spent all her personal concern earlier. She was home, Jenny was safe, someone else was clearly in charge out there.

"Hi." Jenny arrived in the doorway, wearing a long high-necked challis robe with a ruffle at the yoke, long black hair straying about her shoulders. "How was your dinner?"

"Orange duck," said Mary, pithily as concerned that particular restaurant. "If God had intended . . ." It was as foolish not to show a faint reproach as it would be to exhibit anxiety. "You don't seem to have eaten much of yours."

"It's awfully rich," said Jenny defensively. She was eyeing the television set. "There's supposed to be a weird old movie on. Would it bother you . . . ?

"Not at all." Even after a week it was possible at odd moments—as now, when she subsided onto the floor and clasped her arms around her drawn-up knees—to be shocked at Jenny's emaciation. She was probably five-feet-seven; she weighed eighty-odd

7

pounds. The robe seemed in some perverse way to delineate her boniness rather than conceal it, like generous folds slung over a skeleton.

The telephone rang while a list of credits was rolling over the screen to the accompaniment of a sagging sound-track, and Jenny turned an alert face. Mary answered: it was the art director, and as she could tell from his overly hearty tone that he was not alone, she was circumspect in her refusal.

"That's a real disappointment. . . . Well, it was a nice evening anyway, wasn't it? Wonderful dinner."

Obligingly, because Ben was married and had two children and could not afford to be scrupulous about the source of Al Trecino's money or his way with any women in his path, Mary carried out her end of the pretense.

That was at a quarter of ten. The other call came at eleven.

Because of the hour at which she had been advised of her parents' death in the sinking of a cruise ship, Mary had an instinctive distrust of late telephone calls which subsequent years had done little to dispel. Good news, generally speaking, came by day. Late ringings signalled critical illnesses, bare acquaintances wanting to be picked up at the airport, an occasional inebriated friend who thought this would be a good time to come around for a drink.

After she had identified herself to a long-distance operator, her aunt's voice spilled over the wire, low, tense, tumbling. "Mary. Don't let Jenny know I'm calling—she is there, isn't she?"

It was one o'clock in New York. "Yes," said Mary,

8

sounding only cordial and interested in case her cousin's attention had been diverted from the movie. "How are you?"

"He knows where she is," said Henrietta Acton.

Just "he," as if to invoke Brian Beardsley's name would be to give him some occult power. The pace of Mary's heart quickened contagiously: had she locked the door after her when she came in? But that was ridiculous. No matter how furious he was, no thwarted suitor would hope to improve his case by storming the house of someone he had never even met—would he? In Brian Beardsley's case, impossible to tell.

Henrietta was saying distractedly that a friend of Jenny's—"Myrna, Mona, something like that"—had telephoned her earlier, apparently in a fit of remorse, to say that she had allowed Jenny's whereabouts to be coaxed from her. The inference to be drawn was that if Beardsley wasn't already in Santa Fe he was on his way there.

". . . and then some people came in, and I had to wait for Gerald to go to bed because I'm honestly terrified of what this would do to his blood pressure. I'd suggest shipping Jenny home at once, but—well, you know the situation here, and I don't entirely trust this friend anyway. What if it's some kind of trick?"

". . . I see." Mary's mind sped, looking at and discarding possibilities. Try and house Jenny elsewhere for a few days? The only person she felt she could ask that favor of, under the circumstances, was in Europe. Whisk her off to a motel? Any attempt at sequestration would make her suspicious at once,

9

and if Brian Beardsley was really determined to find her, in a city the size of Santa Fe, he could. Jenny was unforgettable to even a casual eye.

"As a matter of fact, I'm not going to be home for the next couple of days," said Mary over the miles, thinking that this was certainly a difficult way to conduct a plot. "I have a cousin visiting me and we're going down to Juarez, just over the Mexican border. Give me a little warning next time, won't you, so that I'll be free?"

"Mary, I'm eternally grateful. Take care."

It wasn't, this time, a casual and empty admonition. "We will, thanks. You too . . ."

Jenny was absorbed in her movie, to all appearances, but the sound was turned low and the telephone was within earshot, and it would have been only natural for her to prick up her ears at the mention of herself. "Did you hear any of that?" asked Mary lightly. "I just put off a visiting acquaintance with a tale about going to Juarez—Cuidad Juarez, officially—and it suddenly struck me that it might be fun."

There was a faint flicker of animation on the narrow face between its curtains of long black hair. "Where's Juarez?"

Mary explained. "It's been dull for you here, and I could use a change myself—I don't know why I didn't think of it before. I've seen a lot of ads for a new motel with a beautiful pool. Why don't you pack, while I see if I can get reservations, because we'll have to leave fairly early in the morning?"

Jenny rose and started out of the room at her

10

dangly marionette gait, saying dubiously, "Mexican *food?*"

"It can be very good, and the black bass is marvelous and so is the shrimp. You won't starve," said Mary, a trifle ironic.

Jenny gave her a brief, aware, over-the-shoulder smile, something she did so seldom that it had the effect of transforming her. The smile widened and brought to life her brooding blue-gray eyes, equipped with the kind of out-spraying lashes generally granted only to horses. She looked like an eighteen-year-old then, instead of an unhappy creature suspended between a scorned childhood and an adult world she had learned to distrust.

In bed, having negotiated successfully with the Casa de Flores, Mary examined a small but puzzling detail. Jenny had reacted sharply both times the telephone had rung, although she had spoken to her parents two nights earlier and they had said they would call next week at the same time. For the first time since her arrival she had been alone for a good part of the evening. Was it possible that the informing Mona or Myrna, covering herself in all directions, had telephoned to let her know that Brian Beardsley was either in or on his way to Santa Fe? Or that Beardsley himself had called?

No, thought Mary to the last. Jenny hadn't been registering anticipation or excitement but something closer to alarm. And, far from placing any obstacles in the way of the projected trip to Mexico, she had looked as pleased as she was currently allowing herself to look about anything.

11

Besides, was it conceivable that she would want anything further to do with Brian Beardsley?

With whom, three months earlier, her stunned parents had discovered her to be having an affair. Apart from the fact that he was twenty-eight to Jenny's eighteen, they knew nothing whatever about him, and upon Jenny's announced intention of marrying him had decided to remedy this situation by quietly hiring a detective service.

Beardsley was not twenty-eight but thirty-two. He had declared himself to be unencumbered, and technically he was, his wife, mother of their two children, having divorced him on the grounds of abandonment. He was a known user of drugs. He had also served a prison term for aggravated assault.

The Actons knew that their only child had a formidable will, but they had assumed that the shock of discovery would offset Jenny's rage at an action she regarded as unforgivable. They were wrong. Beardsley removed himself from the scene, or appeared to, and Jenny virtually stopped eating. Again, her parents regarded this as being as self-correcting as a child's vengefully held breath, and again they were mistaken. While they watched helplessly, her body accustomed itself to a glass of orange juice for breakfast, a half-grapefruit for lunch, a thin slice of meat for dinner.

When she had lost seventeen pounds and her elbows were the widest part of her arms, she went docilely enough to a doctor, who recommended psychiatry. Jenny refused; from the mere fact of diet drinks when she was thirsty, it seemed evident that she had now embarked on a dangerous love affair with her own gauntness.

A new doctor was tried, but he and his predecessor could not agree as to whether this was true anorexia nervosa or, as so often happened in medicine, a close and deluding resemblance. As Jenny's hostility toward her father was implacable under a surface civility—she suspected rightly that he had been the moving force in having Beardsley investigated—the next best choice was to remove her from the battlefield.

The Actons considered their nearby relatives and a few close friends, but they were all too old, or had sufficient problems of their own, or viewed Jenny's behavior with such severity that it was doubtful whether any good could be accomplished. Except for Mary Vaughan, whose twenty-six was not so very far removed from Jenny's eighteen. She had met Jenny on occasional trips East for family weddings and funerals, so that she would not be a complete stranger, and Santa Fe would be a total change from New York.

Mary had realized that any rehabilitation would be a considerable challenge—not unlike walking on water, she thought when she met her cousin at the airport—but she had left her job and she had the time to be friendly chauffeur and cunning cook. She made no mention of Brian Beardsley; if Jenny wanted opinions or advice she would ask for them, and until then either was useless. She prepared dishes like eggs Benedict and chicken Tetrazzini and casseroles with calories numbering in the thousands, and at the end of this first week Jenny's weight had stayed stable and Mary had gained two pounds.

. . . I'll swim night and day in Juarez, she thought, and turned over and went finally to sleep. But her dreams were not pleasant—Al Trecino was in one of them, bearing down on her in his fisherman's sweater—and when, at some unnameable hour, she heard what might have been a car and then the imperative barking of a number of neighborhood dogs, she got up and closed and locked her low-set windows on the chilly, rain-smelling air.

In the morning, it was a minor annoyance to discover that for the third time in the last two weeks a Great Dane puppy newly introduced down the road had made off with her newspaper. He was an engaging animal, frequently not answering to the name of Samuel, and Mary had not been able to bring herself to the point of complaining and possibly getting him tied up. When Jenny, who liked to do the Jumble, came back from her fruitless search and said, "Can we get a paper on the way?" Mary vaguely said yes, if they saw a place, although she had no real intention of stopping for anything once they were under way.

Books, sandwiches to eat in the car as a six-hour drive did not allow for a delaying restaurant lunch even if a restaurant existed without long detours, cold drinks to be nestled in ice in a styrofoam cooler. Mary found herself infected by a superstitious need to hurry, like a burglar knowing that the return of the homeowners was imminent, and wasn't helped by the fact that Jenny had reverted to her detached state and was doing none of the running around. She sat leafing through a magazine in the living room;

14

somehow even her long black hair looked bored.

"Would you take the bags out to the car," said Mary a little briskly, "while I lock up?"

She had considered and decided against telephoning either the Taylors or the Ulibarris, who were her closest neighbors in this fairly isolated area, with the false information that she would be in Palo Alto for a month. When Brian Beardsley came to the house, and Mary was increasingly sure that he would, it seemed somehow wiser for him to be confronted with a blank wall.

Last check: stove off, ashtrays innocent, no faucets dripping. She had already arranged to have the newspaper suspended. Mary locked the front door, carried the books and sandwiches to the car where Jenny was waiting, got in, switched on the ignition. Fifty yards down the road, almost invisible in a weaving of tree shadows, a blue car also came to life. The man in it, grainy-eyed from watching, put the car into gear.

3

. . . He had stared, thunder-struck, at the spindle-legged girl who came out of the house at seven-thirty, wind tugging at the straight dark hair that fell well below her shoulders as she began to saunter along the road-edge, head bent, obviously looking for something.

Had that eternity of hours been for nothing? Had shock and pain . . . ?

No. He refused to be wrong, and everything else fitted. He sat rigid in his nest of shadows, watching and listening, forcing this new factor into place. It wasn't difficult. The woman he was going to execute lived alone—he knew that—and she had listened to the late news, become afraid to spend the night by herself, and recruited a young friend or relative to stay with her. It was fortunate that he hadn't yielded to his impulse at dawn.

In a matter of moments, the skinny dark-haired

one emerged from behind screening lilacs in the next driveway and strolled back the way she had come. The man in the car had already noted that the gate with a wagon-wheel set in it was a gate in name only; it brushed open, a tiny but essential point of corroboration.

The door closed behind her. Five minutes later it opened again, and this time it was the object of his vigil who came out.

For seconds he heard his blood in his ears, a dangerous swish, swish. Short fair hair that cupped her head in a ruffle, as described. The rest of her he observed for himself: slender body, a little over average height, in a green and white dress. A flash of silver plucked off one wrist by the sun as she walked to the car in the driveway at the side of the house, carrying what looked like a cooler. It was a crisp walk, definite, as opposed to her companion's.

The walk of someone who made decisions quickly. Glance through the window at a mortally injured woman seeking asylum, flick out the light, lock the door.

With the rushing sound dying out of his ears and an iciness taking over, he realized in the course of the next fifteen minutes that he was watching preparations for a trip. The fair-haired girl—she was younger than he had expected, and he did not use her name in his brain because it was too soon, it might undermine his control—reappeared with some light-colored garments over her arm, bent into the car with them, went around to the trunk and unlocked it and lifted the lid. Her companion presently trudged out with two suitcases which she hefted inside without apparent difficulty, slamming the lid down again. The fair girl, burdened with a brown paper bag and some books, came out for the last time, locked the door, and proceeded to the car.

He had had time to envision a number of possibilities, including flight, and in fact, partly by chance, he had made one move about that. He had not, however, thought in terms of a passenger—or was she going to drop this one off at her own home, now that her purpose had been served?

He did not lose sight of the car ahead, even though it was overlaid briefly now and then by the vision of his wife's face, so masked in blood that only her teeth and the white of one eye—the other was puffed shut —were visible. The hair he hadn't dared to touch was stiff and crusted.

He still didn't know all of it. He had arrived at his driveway the evening before to find a police car with its roof-light flashing and a deputy in conversation with the driver of a strange pick-up whose headlights were pouring into the trees. Three streets over, the driver had stopped for a woman, obviously the victim of a bad beating. He wasn't familiar with this area and in fact had gotten himself lost, but although she seemed to be in a state of shock the woman had managed to give him her name and her address for the ambulance he was able to summon on his CB radio. She had appeared overcome by fresh terror at the sight of her own driveway, and had only stammered repeatedly, "A boy. He tried to . . ."

She hadn't said anything at all to the ambulance attendant, it was later learned, because she had

18

lapsed into unconsciousness.

They had told him which hospital, and he had reached her in time because forms were still being filled out. Her voice was barely audible, with dazed gaps in it, but he pieced together the facts that she had been outside calling the cat when she was attacked, that she had fought off a knife-assisted attempt at rape, that she had run.

"I don't know where . . ." but there was a rickety bridge over an irrigation ditch, and then a house with nobody home, and next to it a house with a wagon-wheel set in the gate—"I thought it would be latched, but it wasn't, and I fell down . . . and she wouldn't let me in. She looked out the window and turned off the light . . . she locked the door. So I—"

He felt as though his face must be as dark with blood as hers. "What was she like?"

She couldn't seem to grasp what he wanted, because she was wandering through her story like an obedient child and it confused her to be halted. He pressed her, a part of him knowing that this was tantamount to wringing the last few drops out of a sponge, refusing to stop, and she closed her good eye and said, "Young . . . short hair, very blonde." A faltering and effortful gesture with a hand near her own head, a slow welling of tears from under her eyelids. "She locked the door."

They had taken her away to surgery then, and come back not much over an hour later to tell him that they were sorry; there had been too much internal bleeding and she hadn't made it.

The doctor conveying this information had studied his face. "Don't blame yourself for not being at home

19

when it happened. Even if you'd rushed your wife in at once, the damage was done . . . Here, you'd better let me give you something—"

He had turned away from that sop, furiously disbelieving. Hadn't made it—his wife, while he was being eyed furtively by emergency room patients with nothing more wrong with them than bandaged fingers or arms in improvised slings.

He had talked to a city detective then, and made the discovery, not new to countless victims, that there was always an element of official doubt in attempted rape. For example, his wife had known that he would be working late. The detective was sorry to have to ask this question, but it would be vital to their search for her killer. Had they friends aware that she would be alone? Sometimes an evening visit, by invitation or not, was misconstrued, got out of hand . . .

He had restrained himself, already hoarding his hatred because it was clear that the police knew nothing of that failed bid for sanctuary. He pointed out that they had been living in the city for less than a month, and that he did not think that his wife's garb of jeans and one of his old shirts with the sleeves rolled up could be considered provocative. He was spared any more by the entrance of an officer with a wallet incredibly dropped at the scene—during the struggle? Somehow entangled with the knife?

The wallet belonged to a boy out on bond, awaiting trial for the stabbing of a tourist who had declined to give him a cigarette on demand. A factor as incalculable as lightning, and as random in its choice of victim.

He was free to go home then. The cat, Dietrich,

was waiting for him on the front step, sneezing reproachfully, and he did not seize it up and hurl it with back-breaking force against a tree. He let it in, instead, and fed it with a curious gentleness. Without even a glance at the clock he telephoned his sister almost calmly to tell her what had happened, and firmly overrode her suggestion that she and her husband come around at once. He said that he couldn't bear the house at the moment, but would be all right if he went off for a day or two by himself.

Because otherwise the pair of them would take it in turns to be with him every minute, and he could not have that.

His sister had a key to the house, and would undoubtedly be called upon to do whatever had to be done in these instances, and she also had an observant eye. He took a suitcase from the bedroom closet and thrust his shaving kit and some clothes inside, leaving three hangers conspicuously bare and a bureau drawer a little open.

At one point, thinking of a lamp-lit face snapped into darkness, he found himself humming.

His stomach reminded him that he had had nothing to eat since lunch, and he took his ossified dinner from the oven and ate it ravenously before he sat down in the living room with a map of the city spread before him on the coffee table. Dietrich, who had made himself an untidy bed in the yellow knitting, opened his eyes warily at the crackle of paper and then squeezed them tightly shut to render himself invisible; needlessly, because he had been observed without interest.

Three streets over, the driver of the pick-up had

21

said, so here—the tracing finger followed the marked irrigation ditch and paused—was the only place it could be. Sleep now, and then . . . ? But he could not sleep until he had seen and identified the house with the wagon-wheel gate.

He had the night to himself at this hour, and he found the house easily. It was as dark and tranquil as if nothing had happened there; evidently the woman slept, unperturbed. A sudden eruption of barking drove him away somewhat prematurely, but he had accomplished most of his auxiliary mission. Back in his own living room, he took a copy of the city directory from the bookcase and looked up 843 Hounslow Road.

He set the alarm clock then, to allow himself a few hours of sleep. The police knew the name of his wife's assailant, but he had found and would undertake the punishment of her real murderer.

According to the directory, Mary Vaughan.

They were nearly a mile beyond the outskirts of the city when the engine checked, checked again, slowed, and died. Although the symptoms were unmistakable, Mary gazed incredulously at the gas gauge needle standing on zero before she switched off the ignition. She usually took an automatic look at the gauge when there had been any length of time between service-station stops; this morning, with the clear recollection of having the tank filled and the oil and battery checked the day before, she hadn't.

Into the enormous and final silence of a car travelling fifty-five miles an hour and then standing immovable, Jenny asked curiously, "What do we do now?"

All that barking in the night, thought Mary suddenly. Someone had drained her gas tank. It had happened to her once before, and she had meant to buy a cap with a lock, but things not done in the heat of the moment seldom did get done. She had considered, that other time, keeping a reserve can of gas in the trunk, but then envisioned a rear-end collision in which she and the car would go up in a sheet of flame.

"I walk back to a gas station," she said, "and you stay here with the doors locked. It can't be even a mile."

"No, thanks," said Jenny, speedily undoing her seat belt. "We both walk back."

They locked the car. The morning which had felt pleasantly cool was chilly in the blasting wind on the highway, the pebbly shoulder had a faint tilt. It was going to seem a very long walk, thought Mary when they had accomplished perhaps a fifth of it—but here, unmistakably slowing, came one of the vehicles she had half-hoped for: a Volkswagen van, legendary Samaritan of the road. Was it going to turn in at the official-looking building just ahead?

It wasn't. It honked imperatively at a car bumper starting to nose out from under firs and pulled up on the shoulder. The driver, a blond giant with wavy golden hair and a headband, leaned across a girl holding a baby on her lap and glanced from Jenny to Mary. "You in trouble, ma'am?"

Mary explained about her gas, and the boy said cheerfully, "We can give you enough to get you to

Belen. That your car up there? Hop in."

Belen, Spanish for Bethlehem. Mary could feel Jenny's doubt like an actual touch on her arm, but she looked at the scrubbed girl in the Levi shirt, the round-eyed baby, the Irish setter wagging sportively around in the back. She said, "Thank you very much."

Ten minutes and two dollars later, New York-bred Jenny was still disapproving. "They could have robbed us, and then killed us."

"The baby didn't look very dangerous," said Mary mildly.

"A baby would be the perfect ploy."

In view of the theft of her gas, it did not seem the moment to remark that Southwesterners, generally speaking, were quick to respond to people in distress. Mary said instead that with their ringless fingers and casual clothes and unimposing car they scarcely had the appearance of prime targets for robbery in any case.

Jenny, half-turning, made a detached inspection of the simple dress that looked made to order, the bracelet that was an unadorned arabesque of silver, the clear hazel-eyed profile. "You do," she said.

Once back on the road, after the detour for gas and a lock for the tank, Mary began to feel light-hearted and holiday-minded; the ease with which they had gotten through that difficulty seemed an omen. The sun was warmer now, and they would reach the motel in plenty of time for a reviving drink—for her; Jenny was paradoxically prim in that area—and a swim before they did anything else.

24

But she realized presently that it was going to be a very long trip. Jenny asked duty questions—"What are those trees? Was that a roadrunner? Are those the same mountains or new ones?"—but otherwise seemed content to maintain a silence reinforced by her huge sun-glasses. For the first time she could remember, Mary regretted the lack of a radio.

At Socorro, so-named because it was here that a half-starved Spanish expedition had been provided with food by Indians, it seemed time for a sandwich and something to drink. Jenny undid her seatbelt, angled a long bony arm backward, and produced both. She said with a surprised glance at a label, "This isn't diet."

"No." Mary gave her a curious glance. "I can't understand why you want it to be."

This was the closest approach she had made to the situation, and she considered it not only fair but conspicuous by its absence: not to notice someone in Jenny's wasted condition counting calories was like pretending not to see a flowing red beard, grown overnight.

"I like the taste of it," said Jenny, but she had actually hesitated.

She was a neat passenger. She turned presently to tuck the empty cans and wadded-up sandwich bags into the cooler for future disposal. She said casually when she turned back again, "That blue car has been behind us for a long time."

Mary had been intermittently aware of it in the rear-view mirror, but in a day of regulated speed—although most cars on this road nudged sixty and now and then one flashed by at well over seventy—it was possible to travel as far as Las Cruces in a kind of informal convoy. But this was also the loneliest stretch of the journey, with only crows and an occasional circling hawk in the nearby landscape, and the corroboration of the following car made her very slightly nervous. What if Brian Beardsley had simply been keeping an eye on the house for Jenny's emergence?

Well, what if he had? He's served a term for aggravated assault, that's what, thought Mary, and eased the speedometer up to sixty-five. The blue car with its single occupant came along as if on an invisible string, but, again, there were drivers who automatically maintained the speed of the vehicle ahead.

Jenny craned over. "Won't you get a ticket at this rate? I mean if anybody ever patrols this highway?"

She was certainly very law-abiding for someone who had adopted such a rebellious stance over her own affairs—and, like many visitors, she seemed to find the Southwest interesting but a little comical, an area put together amateurishly by well-intentioned people who had not had the advantage of seeing how things were done in the East. "Certainly it's patrolled," said Mary, nettled because it was undeniable that they hadn't seen a single police car in well over two hundred miles. "You didn't think those were real crows, did you?"

At the same time, she flicked on her right indicator and began to move off the road. "Rest area," she said briefly in answer to Jenny's question. "Stretch our legs."

The blue car cruised steadily by, was a heat-shimmered blur, was gone. Still, Mary did a little unhurried strolling around in the wind and sun after she had deposited the lunch litter in a trash can, although Jenny retreated almost at once with defensive hands on her hair, before she got back behind the wheel. They had travelled about five miles when they encountered the blue car again, pulled off in the emergency lane with its flashers on and its hood raised. Its driver, obviously investigating the engine, was visible only as a pair of trousered legs.

Such a sight wasn't at all uncommon on a trip of this length, but Mary wondered that Jenny, who had commented on the car in the first place, made no remark. A fast side glance showed her why: Jenny had dragged her hair over one shoulder and was making her several-times-daily count of her split ends.

They entered a stretch of road where fresh tarring was going on, with flagmen in attendance, and after that a glance at the gas gauge indicated a stop so that they would not have to bother about this particular errand in Juarez. Here, the youth in charge of the hose hung it up when the tank had been filled, proceeded around to the front of the car, bent, straightened, summoned Mary out.

"See that blister?"

Mary bent in turn, but didn't.

"You got a bad soft spot there, that tire could go any time. If it was me, I wouldn't want to take a chance. Matter of fact—" he advanced on the left front tire, squinted, kicked, shook his head "—you got a worse problem there. See that crack?"

Fortunately, from experience and the advice of male friends, Mary knew this approach, used mainly when there were only women in a car although a man wearing coat and tie in the summer could also be considered fair game. She said, "Thank you, I'll have them both taken care of just as soon as I get back to Santa Fe," and observed him taking angry swipes at his hair with a comb as, presently, she pulled away.

There was a new bridge by which to enter Juarez, and she got briefly lost looking for it. Jenny came to life and was told out of Mary's slender store of Spanish that ropas meant clothing and cerveza, beer; she figured out licores by herself. She was astonished at the swarm of tiny tumble-down adobe houses visible on the slope of a hill even before they crossed the border, and the number of people plodding patiently along the foot-walks on the bridge. "Why are there so many of them?"

"Wages are a lot higher in El Paso."

"But some of them are going the other way. Could they smuggle grass?"

Hardly, said Mary, although she had heard of parrots being introduced illegally into the United States by that means. Significant amounts of marijuana came in by planes flying too low for radar observation and making lightning drops in deserted areas. She was having to concentrate on the traffic now, because of the usual bottleneck at Immigration even though obvious tourists were waved through for the price of fifteen cents. She noted automatically that in this gaggle there were a number of blue cars.

Jenny asked curiously, "Can you get out just as easily?"

"Well, not quite." Mary fended off an orange Maverick which was trying to usurp her right of way and leave her stranded while other bumper-to-bumper cars followed it. "If you've spent more than twenty-four hours in Mexico and have luggage, they take a look at it, even though they rely mostly on informers for their real catches. I've never been subjected to an intensive search, but I know people who have."

These questions arose out of natural curiosity about a foreign country, she thought, but for some reason it seemed wise to add, "I wouldn't care to get mixed up with the Mexican authorities in any way. They feel strongly about all kinds of things."

Jenny gazed straight ahead behind her concealing glasses. "I've heard about their jails," she said.

The Casa de Flores justified its name; there seemed to be more flowers, in round and square and oblong beds, than clipped green grass surrounding the cobbled forecourt with Moorish arches and a lot of dark-tinted plate glass. The distances everywhere were silvered by sprinklers and fountains.

Jenny, who seemed to have been expecting something quite different, was visibly impressed. In the huge ornately furnished lobby, Spanish-tiled and almost stumblingly dark to eyes just out of the sunlight, Mary was not so sure. A desk clerk with luxuriant sideburns studied her with admiration just short of a wink, let his gaze roam over Jenny with open astonishment, and continued what was clearly a personal telephone call before hanging up, pushing a registration form across the counter, and presently snapping his fingers at a bellboy. Fast Spanish was used, which had an excluding air.

29

The night before, Mary had asked for and been blandly assured of a room near the pool. She ought to have realized that in hotel parlance "near" was a very flexible word. The fiftyish bellboy conducted them out of the lobby, under one of the arches, up two wide shallow half-flights of stairs, and along a broad and occasionally alcoved corridor of sepulchral chill: "We must be a third of the way home," muttered Jenny over her shoulder. He stopped at one of the planked and pointed doors, produced a key large and heavy enough to serve as a weapon, opened the door with a flourish.

But not before another door, two down and at the end of the corridor, had come snapping open—at the bellboy's burdened tread, the tap of Mary's heels, the slap of Jenny's sandals?—and a man's head emerged. There was something enormously vigilant about this simple action. A cart laden with used plates and glasses and silver reposed outside, which at close to four o'clock would seem to indicate that the occupants were extremely late lunchers or the Casa de Flores was leisurely about cleaning up after room service.

The edge of Mary's vision saw the bellboy lift a semaphoring hand in what was unmistakably a gesture of reassurance. The head down the corridor withdrew itself and the door closed, and she was looking into a room with twin beds, a bureau and desk of carved dark wood, two lamps with enormous shades, two chairs upholstered in turquoise and gold, two paintings of Inquisition-like grimness.

The bellboy said something commanding in Spanish and flung open doors first on a closet and then a bathroom with a long sweep of mirror over a marble counter with inset sink and a great deal of ornamental tile. He gazed expectantly.

"It's very nice," said Mary. "Muy—" but the proper word escaped her, as did the framing of any circumspect query about that apparition down the corridor. Something about the impassive dark eyes, combined with the signal, told her that she wouldn't have learned anything anyway. She tipped the bell-boy, asked for ice, realized that she should have reversed this procedure, turned back into the room to find Jenny gazing at her with respect. "I didn't know you spoke Spanish."

"I don't, beyond about twenty-five words. I keep meaning to take a course, but they have it while I'm having my dinner so one of us will have to reschedule." Now that they were actually here and established, with a suggestion of sufferance in spite of the steep price, Mary felt vacant with fatigue, but she knew that there was something essential missing from the room. Not their suitcases—Jenny was now rummaging through hers and plucking out her bathing-suit—nor the bag containing the Bacardi and limes and fruit juice for which she had stopped at a market on the way . . .

"I'm going to take a shower, unless you want to be first," said Jenny, and Mary stared at her, suddenly transfixed, realizing what she had been failing to find on any of the surfaces in the room. "Our books. I thought we took them out of the car?"

"We did. I put them on top," said Jenny, dawningly anxious because she was a reader too, "while I got our coats. Do you suppose they're still there?"

"Either that or they've been turned in at the desk. I'll call."

But she didn't, at once; even though the books were of the essence because she had only a single half-read paperback in her bag, and she was certainly not going to drive back over the bridge to El Paso for reading matter tonight, Mary felt incapable immediately of a simple, or possibly not so simple in this place, telephone call.

The shower began some tentative starts and stops, as if it had baffling controls, and the bathroom door opened a crack. "Mary? Would you hand me in my shower cap? I think it's in the lid of my suitcase."

"If you'll hand me out half a glass of water." The ice was clearly going to come at a snail's pace, and a drink would have a restorative effect.

Jenny was aghast at the suggestion, but Mary assured her that the water was perfectly safe in places like this. She found the shower cap—pale yellow, frilled at the edge, giving Jenny, who had modelled it for her one evening when she was feeling sportive, a ruffly blonde look at odds with her long introspective face—and the exchange was made.

Mary's Mexico-going knife, useful for peeling fruit from the market, turned up in the bottom of her handbag and she cut a slice of lime to add to her drink. It tasted rewarding indeed after the long drive. The heavy door onto the corridor was not as soundproof as its appearance suggested, because over the rush of the shower Mary could hear a fast incomprehensible interchange of Spanish and then a rattle of china and glasses as the cart outside that other room was towed away.

Who was in it, so extraordinarily watchful and alert? The Mexican divorce laws had been revamped, so that Juarez was no longer a Mecca for film and other celebrities. But possible causes for nervousness would make a long list, and crossing a border was automatically a kind of refuge. Certainly —and here Mary spelled it out for herself—the man was nothing to do with her or Jenny. Henrietta Acton, panicky about her only child and warned by the earlier leakage, would not have mentioned the Juarez trip to anyone at all. And Jenny, ahead of Mary and so with a better look at that out-thrust face, had registered no reaction whatever.

But then, she wouldn't. And she had been completely willing, almost eager to come down here. Mary had to acknowledge the fact, queerly not considered before, that she hadn't the faintest idea what Brian Beardsley looked like.

This was nerves, born of temporary fatigue; she was not one of the ironclad people who could drive for a good part of the day, take a quick shower, and be ready to leap into the local scene. She would have to be careful about imagining Beardsley everywhere; look at her real if fleeting suspicion of the blue car which had followed them so faithfully for so long.

Moreover, that fast assessment from two doors away hadn't seemed in any way personal. It might have been made by someone detached and professional—almost, thought Mary with unknowing irony, a bodyguard.

In Santa Fe, Meg Taylor, in charge of the house while their widowed mother was in the hospital, was

33

saying suspiciously to her younger sister, "I saw you talking to that man this morning. What did he want?"

"What man?" Pippa, who looked at least three years older than her actual fifteen, had lately taken to fluttering her eyelashes at every male who happened her way, and this had led to a number of unwelcome lectures.

"I turned back to put a letter in the mailbox and I saw you," said Meg, grim and insufferable with authority, "and you know how Mom worries about the way you behave. Who was he?"

"I don't know, just somebody looking for that weird girl who's staying with Mary Vaughan," said Pippa, sulky. "She came along early this morning looking for the newspaper after Samuel chewed it up —" at the mention of his name the Great Dane ducked his head coyly, like a dog being complimented "—and I told her we'd try to keep him in tomorrow morning and she said not to bother because they wouldn't be getting a paper, they were going to Juarez. So that's what I told this man, and then, naturally, he asked me to run away with him but I said my sister was in charge of my entire life and I had to get permission first."

"Oh, shut up," said Meg, and, in a fault-finding mood because in spite of her mother's injunctions and her own harangues on the subject she was being stuck with the housework as well as all the cooking, "I shouldn't think you'd hand out information like that to a total stranger."

Pippa rolled her eyes for patience. "Gone to Juarez," she said scornfully. "Big deal."

34

4

How dangerously close he had come to fatal error.

She had gotten farther than he had expected on the very little gas remaining in her tank, which had worked out so well, as he had failed to immobilize her at her house, that it seemed an omen. The outskirts of the city were behind them, the traffic very light, the fir-lined drive of some state building a pure gift when he saw the car falter to a stop on the shoulder.

They would be walking back, and they would be looking into the sun—or if by any chance she had sent her minion to a gas station and remained in the car by herself, that would be even better. But no: there was a distant flicker of color and motion between chinks in the firs.

Here they came, Mary Vaughan fortuitously on the outside. He said her name to himself often now; that barrier was not only down but trampled upon. If he had spoken it aloud, it would have had a crooning inflection.

He mustn't let them get too close, as he would have to gather a killing speed. He glanced to his left: nothing coming. He reminded himself about impact—he had once hit a large dog and the resulting jar had been considerable—and put the car in motion.

Blare.

Out of nowhere, light gray against the light gray highway, came a Volkswagen van, slowing, stopping with only one possible purpose—and when Mary Vaughan had been close enough for her voice to have been audible if it hadn't been for the wind. He struck the rim of the steering-wheel bruisingly hard with his fist.

The Volkswagen's engine revved noisily and then receded, leaving the roadside empty. His head had cleared enough for a mordant thought. Mary Vaughan had all the earmarks of an attractive young woman, and angels of mercy did not always turn out to be that. Wouldn't it be funny if . . . ? No, it wouldn't be funny. She belonged to him alone; in a way she was as much his possession as his wife had been.

He waited five minutes, ten, got out of the car and peered around the edge of the firs. Even at that distance the clear air showed him when the driver of the van came into view, the transfer of gas evidently complete, and climbed into it and drove off.

Mary Vaughan would almost certainly go into Belen, the nearest town, for a fill-up—and she turned off at the first exit. He didn't follow her, in case any of the paintwork had shown when he started out of the drive, and he was confident that the cooler indicated a destination beyond that. Again he waited, and she reemerged onto the highway in about twenty minutes. He settled down to what he suspected would be a long drive, quite glad now of the Volkswagen's intervention. She wouldn't have known what struck her, literally, and that was scarcely fair. She must be allowed time to know what was about to happen to her, and to plead.

Her pull-off at the rest area worried him briefly, but he reasoned that she was consulting a map or simply taking a break from driving, because the time to turn back—knowing herself to be a murderess, suddenly aware of being followed, deciding to go to the police for protection—would have been at Belen. He drove on for a few miles before he stopped, raised the hood of the car, ate the sandwich he had bought at the diner where he had had breakfast, with the knowledge that this day might take a peculiar shape, drank the accompanying carton of cold black coffee.

With the coffee, because one of the headaches that had so disturbed his wife was beginning to clamp around the base of his skull, he took a tranquilizer.

When his rear-view mirror showed him a dot in the heat-shimmer he pulled on his flashers, got out of the car, prepared to lean invisibly in over the engine. His quarry drove past him, but so, by the time he had thumped the hood down and gotten back behind the wheel, did a huge semi, rocking him in its wake as it roared by, flanked in the other lane by a camper.

After all those empty miles it was like having a cliff rear up ahead. The camper hung just behind the truck's left rear wheel, not allowing an opening, and when he moved over behind it and sounded his horn the driver extended his arm in a severe, palm-down waggle.

He saw the Las Cruces exits go by, but each time the gray bulk obscured the ramps. Presently the semi commenced to slow, but as it was still travelling over the speed limit the camper stayed in position. They proceeded in a locked-in trio almost as far as the truck weighing station, and when the distance was visible again he was almost furious enough to try to drive the camper off the road as he shot by it.

She had vanished.

Was she tooling around some unfindable side street in Las Cruces right now, bound for the home of a friend or relative? The stale sandwich bunched in his stomach at the thought, the coffee echoed in his throat. It had become clear to him—when?—that Mary Vaughan had to be dead by the time his wife was buried. That, and that alone, would carry him through the funeral.

On a frontage road, a gas station came into view, the first in well over a hundred miles. Was there a chance—? He needed gas, whatever he decided to do. He swung onto the apron in front of a row of pumps, asked a boy with a greasy pompadour to fill the tank but skip the oil and battery, said when the boy came back from a measuring look at his front tires, "I gave a lady a hand about ten miles back, she was having trouble with her butterfly valve and said she was going to stop at the first place she saw. I wonder if she came through here?"

He described the car and, out of indelible memory, the green-and-white dress. "There was a young girl with her, skin and bone, with long dark hair." He triggered a response he couldn't have hoped for.

"Yeah, but all she wanted was gas and the key." He jerked his head backward at the sign indicating a ladies' room. "The kid with her, a real freak like you say, stuck her head out the window and said—" here there was a falsetto mince, accompanied by hand on hip "—'Is it as hot as this in Juarez?' "

Handed to him on a platter. He nodded indifferently over his leap of exultation, paid, drove away.

Juarez. He was familiar enough with the city to know that out of its many motels only three or four would appeal to Mary Vaughan and friend; he was, in fact, reasonably sure which one would be at the top of the list. He wondered a little about that lapse on the dark girl's part—but then, how anxious would Mary Vaughan have been to impart the real motive behind this trip, and the necessity for keeping her tracks well covered?

What she had done was not easily confessable.

There were a couple of essential items missing from the suitcase he had packed so providentially to avoid his sister's solicitude, but there would be time enough to acquire those once he knew where Mary Vaughan had gone to ground.

He chose the fastest bridge. He did not get lost.

"Libros," repeated Mary doggedly to the desk clerk. She was making the discovery that the Casa de Flores was carelessly run under its surface pomp, and that when any smallest difficulty arose the staff elected, or had been instructed, to retreat behind a language barrier. She patted the air at shoulder height. "Mi carro."

She had already been out to the car, parked humbly between a Continental and a Cadillac, and there was no sign of the books, three hardcover and three paperback, either there or on the surrounding cobblestones. Even apart from the pressing problem of something to read, because Juarez was innocent of English-language novels, they were books she wanted back. She also had a suspicion that the clerk had a perfectly good grasp of English, and was enjoyably watching her make a fool of herself.

She said crisply, changing her tactics, "When we arrived this afternoon, I put some books on top of my car while we were getting other things out, and they aren't there now."

The clerk studied her with keen attention as she spoke, as though he were a lip-reader, and then swept an arm around his small domain. He said, deliberately approximating her own command of Spanish, "You see? No books."

"Then would you ask the bellboy, please?"

This brought a frown of impatience, much as if Mary ought to do her reading at home and not bother the clerk with it. He glanced around the lobby, consulted his watch, pulled out a sliding board evidently containing a schedule of some kind. "I am sorry." He had clearly lost interest in the whole business and become intrigued with someone behind Mary. "Alfredo is not now on duty."

"Can you tell me when he will be on duty, then?" Not for anything would she glance around. "I really must have those books back."

The clerk shrugged, implying that this was as

chancy as predicting earthquakes. "Nine o'clock?" he suggested.

There was nothing to do but accept defeat for the time being. Mary asked to be informed if her books turned up before the bellboy did, and left the desk with a casual look at what had so bedazzled the clerk. He wasn't entirely to be blamed: it was a tall dark commanding woman in a gold sari, with a small but brilliant diamond fastened in her left nostril.

Strange, she reflected, going in search of Jenny and the pool and a swim of her own, the number of people who seemed to equate arrogance with elegance. The forecourt was crowded with cars, most of them costly, and their owners could not all be experimenters like herself; the Casa de Flores had been open for several months. It was considerably more expensive than other motels here, but the front-desk attitude, which generally reflected policy, appeared to be that guests should not trouble the management; they were lucky to be here at all.

A sound of splashing at the end of a tiled corridor led Mary to the pool. It was vividly blue, not much short of Olympic size, with the usual sprinkle of umbrella-shaded tables and, for the preponderance of people who came to pools for display or tanning purposes, long recliners. There was paging as well as bar service, because as Mary emerged into sunlight a voice rendered flat and atonal by travelling across water said, "Miss Beryl Oates, please, Miss Beryl Oates."

As always when it was clear that a page was going to be unanswered, Mary was fleetingly tempted to identify herself as Miss Beryl Oates. What exotic messages were intended for these elusive people? "Air India has confirmed your reservation to Nepal"? "The judges were unanimous in their choice of yours as the prize-winning entry"? "Bring home a can of tomato soup"?

By five-thirty the warm gold of the sun was false, the air turning faintly crisp. The only people in sight were two children splashing in the roped-off shallow end of the pool, an elderly man in dark glasses recumbent on a long chair, and, at one of the umbrella-sheltered tables, Jenny.

Oddly, she looked less startling in her one-piece claret bathing-suit than she did in conventional attire. Sitting negligently on the end of her spine, all long milky arms and legs, black hair trailing, she might have been a water nymph, naturally not of the same dimensions as mortals. On the table beside her bathing-cap was a glass of iced tea, half full. Across from it was another glass, and an empty Carta Blanca bottle.

"How's the water?" inquired Mary, and Jenny glanced up with a visible start; she had been unaware of any approach. "Oh—nice, but on the chilly side. If you're going in, I ought to warn you that there's a lot of chlorine."

Which, curiously enough, had left the whites of her eyes unaffected. I'm not going to pry about her beer-drinking companion, thought Mary, but neither am I going to be chased away from the pool. She said lightly, "I'll get wet, at least," and took her cap from her pocket, unzipped the towelling robe, walked to the pool edge, and dived in.

The water was, as Jenny had said, extremely cool. Mary couldn't detect any odor or sting of chlorine (although someone had told her that alkali was actually to blame for any irritation). It was the first time she had swum since the summer before, and she was breathless after a single fast trip down to the float-bobbing rope and back again. Here she found Jenny, now muffled in white terry, standing on the concrete deck, gazing down at her and saying, "I think I'll go up to the room and write some postcards, okay? Have you got the key?"

"In the pocket of my robe." Luckily, they were very deep pockets. Mary swam away again, wondering, a little worried. Was Jenny, whom she had hoped would enjoy this necessitous trip, regarding her as a chaperone, checking up? How to reassure her that if she had found some friendly man—and for some reason Mary felt sure it was a man—that was all to the good?

Unless the man was someone Jenny didn't want her to know about. Like Brian Beardsley. But even if he had arrived in Santa Fe, even if by some kind of second sight he had discovered their departure for Juarez, he couldn't possibly have pinpointed the Casa de Flores so soon.

Except that it was the newest motel in Juarez, cleverly masquerading as a resort. If he had asked someone about a good place to stay, he might very well have been directed here.

A part of Mary's mind saw Jenny upstairs, not writing postcards but at the telephone asking hurriedly to be connected to another room. Another sector remembered those two gained pounds—no, more, consider those snappy-cheese-and-green-pepper sandwiches on the way down here, while she did nothing more active than keep a foot on the accelerator and make minute corrections with the steering-wheel.

By now, the water felt warmer than the air. Mutinously, with a goal of fifteen laps, Mary went on swimming.

For some hours, the Santa Fe police had had their murder suspect in custody on grounds of suspicion, but if he succeeded in obtaining the services of the attorney he had asked for, he wouldn't be there long. This attorney would cry discrimination because of a Spanish surname, and ask incredulously if anyone seriously believed that his client, out on bond while awaiting trial, would have been so stupid as to place himself in further jeopardy?

Certainly the suspect did not look stupid; his pointed face had the alertness of a snake's. Picked up with surprising ease at his parents' home, the address on his driver's license, he said that his wallet had been lifted the day before while he was playing pool. Had he reported the loss of his license? Shrug; he was going to get around to it.

Where had he been last evening between seven-thirty and eight o'clock? With friends; he produced names, confidently. In view of the nature of the dead woman's injuries it was impossible that her attacker could have walked away without bloodstains; could they see his clothing? They sure could. He showed them notably clean jeans and a flowered shirt, and when a deputy walked into the kitchen and remarked that the washing machine was set on "Cold" he said, "Haven't you heard about the energy program, man?" and pointed down at a large box of cold-water detergent. "Bio-degradable," he said with a grin.

What were those purple bite-marks on his thumb? He'd been fooling around with the dog, he said, and snapped his fingers for the animal; it cowered.

There was no use trying to get anything out of his parents, who had summoned the police a few months earlier on an occasion when he had attacked them with his fists. There must have been reprisals for that, because even with the police now present they were clearly terrified of their son.

As the attack had taken place in the driveway, there was no hope of fingerprints. Footprints were also out, as the ground had been dry for a couple of weeks; the rain hadn't started until about a quarter of eight. Grass under the trees gave them blood but nothing else.

The driver who had stopped for the victim had been requestioned, but without further result. All she had said was, "A boy. He tried to . . ." and the obvious inference there was attempted rape. Same with the ambulance attendant and at the hospital, which wasn't odd: even without severe physical damage leading to shock, women tended to try to block this thing out.

According to her husband, whose innocence was unmistakable on a number of grounds, she hadn't said anything helpful in the few minutes he had with her before she died. "She described running, trying to get away, but we're fairly new here and it was dark and she had no idea where she was. And of course she was—well, pretty incoherent . . ."

But she must, the police reasoned, have tried to find refuge somewhere between her driveway and the street where she had been picked up. There were houses, after all; it wasn't as if she had been staggering about a deserted mesa. What had happened there?

They would have to try to trace her route. More importantly, they would have to find the weapon, whose dimensions the police surgeon had been able to give them with fair accuracy because of that killing plunge. It wasn't in the suspect's home; they had established that, and it wasn't anywhere in the vicinity of the attack.

But here they had a slight break. A friend of the suspect's, hauled in routinely because he was known to the police for a variety of reasons, thought correctly that they would overlook the very small amount of marijuana in his possession at the time if he gave them any assistance. He said positively, "No way he'd throw away that knife, man, he loved that thing. He's got it stashed somewhere he can get at it."

So, find the knife.

Six blocks away, a mortuary assistant, having mistaken the deceased's brother-in-law for her husband and been set right about this, was exhibiting caskets with the briskness of a sporting-goods salesman even though he was a little deflated because the best sales were to the nearest and dearest. "Now, a lot of people like this one. Oak, simple but nice if you know

46

what I mean. Of course, the lining isn't quite as luxurious as—"

"My brother wants the casket closed," said Eunice Howe firmly, thereby disposing of the lining, and the assistant gave her an indulgent look. People never realized the wonders that could be performed cosmetically on even the most battered face. Indeed, he often thought that those laid out looked better than they had while walking around, what with tasteful hair arrangements and makeup and so on. He started to say something delicate about this, but Mrs. Howe cut him short by making a brisk choice and then giving him her telephone number although, she said, her brother would be in touch with him about any further arrangements.

"Not that I think he will," she remarked to her husband as they emerged from organ-sounding dimness onto a gravelled walk. "When I talked to him he sounded in an absolute state of . . ."

She frowned at herself, exploring for the right word. ". . . shock," she finished, and instinctively kept to herself the fact that that wasn't really what she had meant at all.

5

It was a quarter of seven when the doorknob turned almost soundlessly for the first time.

On returning from the pool, Mary had found Jenny writing postcards as announced—one, she couldn't help noting, to a Myrna Vetch in New York. But postcards travelled almost at a walking pace; it wouldn't matter.

She had then taken a speedy shower, made a second and this time successful request for ice, fixed herself a drink, and squeezed lime into papaya juice for Jenny. Although not normally given to much viewing, she found herself longing for a television set, even of the caliber usually found in motels: it would have allowed them to husband their tiny supply of reading matter. As things were, she was trying to follow her own advice to Jenny and dwell on every word twice when something made her glance at the door and its tentatively swivelling knob.

48

She was out of her chair at once, calling in a clear voice, "Yes? Who is it?" but by that time there was the sound of a key entering the lock. It seemed imperative to reach the door and open it before it could be opened from the outside. Mary managed this, heart beating much faster than at any time during her swim, and confronted a green-uniformed chambermaid. Down the corridor, another door closed quietly.

"Is there something you want?"

The woman, slender and unusually tall for her race, shook her cropped dark head in obvious incomprehension. Under ordinary circumstances Mary would have been able to produce at least an operative word or two of Spanish; now, for the first time in her life, she was powerless to communicate with another human being, and it was almost as dismaying as losing the faculty of speech itself.

She had taken an automatic step backward, as if to make way for the passage of towels or other paraphernalia, and the maid walked past her and into the room. She detoured around Jenny, who was pressed back in her chair like a silent statement of fear, bent a little from the waist, commenced a slow, intent, downward-staring prowl at the foot of the far twin bed and then the space between that and the wall.

"I think we're looking for something," said Mary casually, to break the spellbound quiet.

"I think we're off our rocker," said Jenny, barely audible, but the alarm had gone out of her; she was now simply amazed and diverted. As though sensing herself to be the object of a wondering discussion, the maid turned, divided a glance between them, tugged

49

at an ear lobe, shrugged. Mary spread her hands and shook her head to indicate that they hadn't found an earring, and the maid withdrew as mutely as she had entered.

"My *God,*" said Jenny in awe when the door had closed. "Do they just walk in like that down here?"

Once again, and for no good reason, Mary was defensive. "Someone in this room before us obviously lost an earring, and may be accusing the maid. She's probably worried about her job." Might as well go ahead on this tide of crispness. "Is something worrying you, Jenny?"

Jenny gave her a wide and apparently candid blue-gray glance. "Look," she said practically. "I'm just getting over Indians, and here you introduce me to Mexicans. I'm sure they're friendly and courteous and everything you say, but it's kind of weird when you don't understand a word of their language, and that woman would give anybody the creeps."

Mary, getting dressed to go to dinner, acknowledged to herself that Jenny had indeed exhibited a surprisingly childish fear of Indians, whether selling handmade jewelry from their blankets along the plaza or shopping in supermarkets, some of the men with their hair tied back, the women in voluminous layers of skirts and soft, soundless boots. And it was true that the chambermaid had been briefly unnerving.

But there had also been something sharply personal in Jenny's reaction, almost like that of someone shown, without warning, the photograph of a dangerous face.

*   *   *

50

They did not have dinner at the Casa de Flores. At the entrance to a very dark dining room with a number of vacant tables, all with reserved signs although it was early for dinner in Mexico, the headwaiter suggested suavely that perhaps they would care to have a drink in the bar while they waited? Mary, who resented being manipulated in this blatant fashion, declined, and only realized when they were seated in a restaurant within easy walking distance that Jenny hadn't wanted to leave the motel.

It was too late by then—they had already ordered boquilla black bass—but Mary wondered suddenly if there hadn't been altogether too much pussyfooting with this half-child, half-woman. She said directly, "Jenny, if you've met someone at the motel why didn't you say so, for heaven's sake, and we could have stayed there for dinner? I thought we ought to leave on principle, but my principles are easily bent in a good cause."

For the first time, Jenny looked so flustered that her eyelashes seemed in danger of getting tangled. "Oh, no. I hate that too, drumming up business for the bar," she said, and then, selecting a tostado, "What do I do with this?"

Change of subject. Mary indicated a small bowl of chili. "You dip it in that," she said, "but cautiously. I have a friend who mistook it for vegetable soup two years ago, and people still ask him why he's crying."

Jenny did as advised and winced only a little, perhaps because her mind was on something else. She lifted her gaze to Mary in open curiosity. "Speaking of meeting people, how come—I mean, you're so attractive—you aren't engaged or anything? Oh," she said to herself in rebuke, "that is *rude.*"

Mary was entertained at the "or anything." "No, it isn't. I'm twenty-six, and I was engaged, about a year ago. We decided to call it off by mutual consent."

Jenny, having introduced a subject which might be regarded as somewhat personal, appeared to have lost interest; her glance was absorbed in something else.

"He thought he ought to have his ring back," continued Mary in exactly the same tone, "but I fooled him by swallowing it. Heated words were exchanged, I'm sorry to say."

Jenny heard none of this. "Well, you have an admirer now," she said. "Behind and to your left, sitting by himself under that mirror with all the decorations. He hasn't taken his eyes off you since he came in."

Their dinner arrived as she was speaking, wheeled up on a cart, the bass boned and served with the flourishes usually associated with crêpes suzette. Mary turned her head to thank the waiter and ask for two Carta Blancas, and in the same motion let her gaze rove a casual few degrees.

And removed it at once from the man seated alone at a table against the wall, because holding his regard, very light in a tanned face, was like holding on to one end of a rubber band stretched to snapping point. Mary said distractedly to Jenny, "There's tartar sauce, but try the bass with just lime first," and realized too late that there were a lot of calories in tartar sauce.

"Who is he?" asked Jenny, contriving a hiss as she picked up a wedge of lime. "Someone you know, or a visiting wolf?"

"I have no idea. You can eat the salad in places like this, the lettuce comes from El Paso," said Mary earnestly—why was it that all natural conversation fell dead at moments like this?—while she went on feeling that steady contemplation on the back of her head.

Or . . . ? For the first time she became aware of a length of mirror half-dividing the dining room into two sections and holding her own small but clear reflection: slightly peaked brows, a touch of sunburn on her cheekbones, hair almost as gold, in this light, as the heishi earrings sewing an occasional sparkling stitch on the air. In the rear distance, the perfectly stilled sleeve and shoulder of a dark coat.

Mary did not glance at the mirror again, because if the man behind her shifted his chair slightly she would find him in it too. She talked determinedly to Jenny, asking about distant and half-forgotten relatives and realizing resentfully that she was scarcely even enjoying the black bass, which was sweet and delicate, or experiencing any triumph over the fact that Jenny liked and drank the Mexican beer—for which she proceeded to compensate by ignoring her baked potato and refusing dessert.

True to his calling, the waiter who had asked twice if everything was satisfactory presented the check and vanished, apparently forever. Rather than remain in her spotlit position, Mary put down bills that left him far too big a tip. Their progress toward the door took them necessarily past the table for two against the wall, and the man there came to his feet as they approached.

"My name is Daniel Brennan," he said, offering his

hand to Mary, "and if you caught me staring it's because I'm always surprised to see another Santa Fe face down here." He seemed to be visited briefly by doubt. "You are Mary Vane, aren't you? Someone introduced us at an affair at the La Fonda—Willie Wilkinson, I think."

Mary corrected her last name politely and introduced Jenny. If only he had come over to their table and said that earlier, she thought.

"I think they've gone out to search for a boat to catch my shrimp," said Brennan. "Won't you—" he cast a glance around for another chair "—sit down and have a cordial?"

Up close, his gaze wasn't formidable at all but merely an extremely light gray. "Thank you, but we have to be getting back," said Mary, and was asked inevitably where they were staying. Told the Casa de Flores, Brennan said, "I'm meeting a friend there tomorrow, a business colleague really, so perhaps I'll see you again?"

It seemed an actual question rather than the usual automatic courtesy, and Mary said yes, perhaps, and added a goodnight. Outside in the half-dark—this part of the city contained a kind of exhaled light at all hours, as if the pale shop-fronts around the huge plaza had stored up some of the fierce white sun—it struck her as odd that after his introduction to her Daniel Brennan hadn't so much as glanced at Jenny again. Delicacy, because in her sleeveless teal-blue dress she looked more than ever like an X ray of herself?

Somehow Mary thought not, and a very peculiar idea had entered her head. The motel pool was lit,

54

throwing up a muted flare of green-gold, and although the night was cool Jenny got into her still-damp bathing-suit. "I love swimming at night, and I have to work off that beer," she said with friendly mockery. "Are you coming?"

"Maybe just to watch you—I think I'll go into the matter of our books first," said Mary, sitting down on the bed near the telephone. "Incidentally, should you be swimming so soon after dinner?"

"That's an old wives' tale," said Jenny, and departed.

Mary did not pick up the receiver and ask if Alfredo had returned to his station. She didn't remember ever having been introduced to Daniel Brennan, and his was a decisive-featured face. The La Fonda was a safe choice as background, because most large functions in Santa Fe were held at the old hotel, and Willie Wilkinson as agent even safer: tirelessly social and insatiably curious, he seemed to have mastered the trick of being everywhere at once.

But if this story were false, how had Daniel Brennan known her name, with that slight and convincing inaccuracy?

Jenny's parents had met Brian Beardsley, and could tell Mary his approximate height and his general appearance even if, say, a mustache had been removed or hair color altered. While she waited through the expected complications of putting a call in to New York from Mexico, Mary examined the possible reasons that would make Beardsley pursue Jenny at all.

Genuine love, when he had lied to her in essential areas? A determination to reinvolve her with him as revenge against the Actons for having had him investigated? Or, very simply, money? Gerald Acton would not qualify for a wealthiest-men list, but Henrietta had money of her own and their son-in-law could look forward to a well-upholstered future. For all their thunder and lightning, they would never disinherit their only child.

Of all these motives, Mary liked the second least, because, on the record, Brian Beardsley was not a man to provoke. And it had to be considered that persuading Jenny back into an affair or even marriage was not the only or the worst way he could hurt the Actons.

And what about Jenny, deliberately calling Mary's attention to the fact of a watcher in the restaurant: was she capable of such guile? Yes. Mary didn't even have to weigh the question. She had the fierce, single-minded commitment of her age to what she looked upon as inviolable rights, Beardsley's as well as her own, and it would undoubtedly give her a good deal of satisfaction to outwit the system. She was, at least now, of a peculiarly unyielding nature; she did not have that brooding look for nothing.

. . . Mary realized that the Actons' telephone was finally ringing—and ringing, and not answering.

She sat for a few moments with her hand on the cradled receiver, staring reflectively at it, and then she left the room, locked the door, turned to see a waiter emerging from the small service elevator with a laden cart. Dinner for two in the room at the end of the frigid corridor. What could it be like in winter?

Although the courtyard was now a packed glisten of cars, the only people Mary encountered on her way to the pool were the Indian woman, tonight resplendent in a sari of deep blue bordered with silver, and a gray-haired delegation wearing oblong plastic name tags and expressions of daring gaiety, as if, safely away from home, they might engage in a hat dance later in the evening. The women with their short curls and ruddy skins and pant-suits looked curiously like the men, or perhaps it was the other way around.

At first glance, the brilliant, still-shaking pool was empty. Then Mary, eyes adjusting to darkness made blacker by contrast, saw the hand holding onto the deck at the deep end; saw, too, a figure crouched there, an arm going out and down as she watched.

She called sharply, "Jenny?" as she walked closer, and the arm withdrew, what was now identifiably a man came to his feet and moved away without hurry, Jenny's white-capped head appeared as she lifted herself on her elbows. The dazzle behind her made it impossible to read her expression, but Mary had a feeling that it was annoyed.

That couldn't be helped—and she was, after all, the cause of these uneasy speculations. Mary said, bending toward the lifted face, "Jenny, when your parents talked to you on Tuesday night did they say anything about going away in the next few days? I just tried to reach them, to let them know where we are, and I don't want to keep trying if there's no point."

"My mother said they might go to the Cape if the weather was decent." Jenny shifted the position of her hands, braced her feet against the side of the pool, pulled her body into a bow. "You don't need to worry about them calling till next week, anyway. You should see my father when the telephone bill comes in."

My mother. My father. Had she always placed them at that cool biological remove? The crouching man hadn't taken himself very far away after all; an edge of Mary's vision saw him drop down onto a chair at the table where Jenny had sat that afternoon. In the brief wink of a struck match, there was even what looked like a bottle of Carta Blanca there again, and a glass.

Jenny was now pulling herself forward and back in the water, clearly impatient for Mary to depart so that she could get on with her swim. Or just for Mary to depart?

The feeling, once again, of coming along like a wardress to spoil things for her cousin gave Mary a faint crispness. "Look, Jenny, it was my idea to come down here and I really think your parents should know, just in case. Your mother must have said where on the Cape they might be going."

"Well, their best friends, the Mitchells, have a summer place there—you must have met them, nobody in the family can get married or buried without them. He's a sailing nut, I think he sleeps in his blazer, and . . ."

Was Jenny being purposely maddening? As though aware of a certain irritation above her, she went on hastily, "They open up their house in Wellfleet around now, but they never get around to having the telephone connected until everything else is done because otherwise people descend on them in droves, so if I were you," she was either matter-of-

58

fact or slightly amused, "I'd just stop worrying about it."

So much for obtaining a description of Brian Beardsley, who, although it couldn't be true, summoned up a vision of brown hair, old tweeds, a calm way with a pipe. Mary left the pool area, marvelling that neither she nor Henrietta had thought of this in the course of that alarmed and alarming telephone call. But the weather-permitting Cape visit had been projected before her aunt learned of the new turn of events; would they still have gone ahead with it? Very probably. With the feeling of a problem solved and danger averted, people tended to heave a sigh of relief and proceed as planned.

There was a different clerk at the desk. He was not much of an improvement on the old. He said disbelievingly, *"Books?"* as if there could be no possible use for such objects at the charming, diverting Casa de Flores, and after that he implied that the motel could scarcely be responsible for Mary's carelessness, but he wrote something on a memo pad. "I will send Alfredo to you," he promised.

Like that first consignment of ice, Mary thought disenchantedly.

The Casa de Flores came to life in the evening; from two cavelike, lantern-lit bars issued muted sounds of revelry and mariachi music, chopped into almost-silence by the closing of the heavy glass doors of the lobby. The lawns and flowers, floodlit, looked vivid and unreal, something to be rolled up and stored for the night when everybody had gone to bed. Mary walked to the proper arch and mounted the steps, hearing an echo in the encroaching cold.

It wasn't an echo, it was someone behind her, and this was no time to think about the recessed alcoves spaced along the corridor, holding huge urns of sand and their own darkness. She turned casually as she took her room key from her bag, and—something about the way he moved? The shape of his face in that quick flare of match-light?—knew that this was the man from the pool.

His features were not obscured now, and she half-caught her breath and almost spoke.

6

But the message that had flashed through her senses was wrong. This was not, by one of the wild coincidences the world was full of, the man she had mentioned to Jenny so lightly at dinner, the man she sometimes missed astonishingly. Apart from a certain angularity of cheekbone, and the way his hair grew at his temples, he didn't resemble Spence at all.

In spite of this instant realization, Mary was still a little off-balance when he said pleasantly, producing his own key, "Your young friend is a remarkable swimmer. Competition material, if she'd work on her turns."

Friend. Not surprisingly, at her age and in her circumstances, Jenny hadn't wanted to be labelled as in the company of any relative, even a cousin, and in fact Mary, out of some intuition, had merely said to Daniel Brennan, "This is Jenny Acton." And this man had heard the trace of alarm in her voice as she neared the pool, and was politely explaining himself and his attentions away.

"She is, isn't she?" said Mary, polite in turn, and was about to use her key when she became aware that he was studying her face intently, as though making up his mind whether to add something else.

He did. He said, "I'm afraid this will sound intrusive, but Jenny seems like a very nice girl and I wondered—she told me this afternoon that she lives in the East—if her parents had ever heard of Dr. Bechstein, in Denver? The reason I ask is because I have good friends with a daughter in pretty much her condition, and he's been able to do a lot for her."

Mary, growing instinctively stiff, knew that this approach from a stranger was not really astonishing. A great many people came to New Mexico for the relief of physical ills—arthritis, or asthma or other respiratory problems—and concerned sympathy, particularly from those who had encountered successful treatment, crossed lines usually drawn. Too, in spite of her flashes of irony, Jenny often showed the vulnerability of a child. But although Mary had been disowned to a degree she was still not going to discuss Jenny's problems with someone encountered sixty seconds ago.

She said a little aloofly, "I'm sure her parents—" and broke off and turned instinctively, following his sharpened gaze over her shoulder. At the end of the corridor, motion so fast that she had just missed it indicated the withdrawal of a watcher there.

"They've Got a Secret," observed the man in audible quotes. He weighed his key tentatively, took a step backward, patted his pockets, said, "Left my cigarettes behind," and smiled at Mary. "Good night."

Mary responded mechanically, watched him disappear around the turn for the stairs, let herself into her room. A peculiar tingly feeling remained from that first shock; she had to remind herself that it was not Spence uttering Jenny's name so warmly.

Five minutes later, at a signalling tap, she opened the door to her cousin, who looked flushed and bright-eyed if a bit shivery in her terry robe, and wanted to know if Mary was contemplating a bath right away, because otherwise she was going to wash her hair.

"Go ahead," said Mary, now accustomed to this frequent process, and watched with interest while the contents of a zippered makeup case were disinterred. There were three plastic bottles and a tube, all evidently designed to cope with the Great Split End Crisis. She said casually, curious as to the reaction, "I met your pool friend. He thinks that with a mustache you'd be another Mark Spitz."

She was instantly appalled at herself; why had she put it that way? Jenny stared briefly, and the stare was not friendly. Mary said rapidly, "That was my own translation. What he actually said was that you're a marvelous swimmer, you could compete, and he thinks you're very nice."

Although it was exactly what he had said, it acquired a faintly patronizing flavor in the conveying, but Jenny didn't seem to mind. She collected a lock of her black hair and draped it experimentally over her upper lip. "Come to that, I saw your Mr. Brennan downstairs. Spying out the territory for tomorrow, would you say, or panting for another glimpse of you?"

We're needling each other, thought Mary in amazement. I like her, and I think she likes me, but listen to us. She jumped up. "I brought bath powder, if you didn't. Wait a second and I'll get it for you."

It was a fragrance Jenny had admired. Mary picked up her book when the bathroom door had closed and the ablutions begun, but although it was a very good English mystery novel she did not immediately plunge herself into it again. "Your Mr. Brennan," Jenny had said—but something in that brief interchange at the restaurant, although she had not realized it until now, had rung slightly false.

"I'm always surprised to see another Santa Fe face down here," Daniel Brennan had said as an excuse for his dwelling regard, but, apart from Texans, New Mexicans formed the largest bloc of U.S. visitors. In the course of one weekend the autumn before, while staying at another motel, Mary had seen three people she recognized.

Firmly, she resumed her book, wishing that it were possible for her to like steak-and-kidney pie.

The pool area was deserted, and the underwater light had been switched off.

The man on the concrete deck had been holding his right hand in the water for over five minutes. Two fingers had been frostbitten when he was a boy, and even after all these years any prolonged exposure to cold turned them a startling tallow color, the nails tinged with blue. People tended to comment on it.

He took his hand out of the water, straightened,

used his handkerchief and walked away from the pool, lighting a cigarette for anyone who might be watching although curtains were drawn everywhere. Carelessly, a guest taking a stroll before retiring or entering one of the bars for a nightcap, he passed under one of the lanterns directing the way back and glanced at his hand.

As he had hoped, he would not draw any attention to himself if he decided to use the pool. His middle fingers had not turned white.

At something after ten o'clock, Mary gave up on the recovery of her books.

Her swim had revived her briefly that afternoon; so, later, had drinks and dinner. Now, all at once, the various encounters of the day had her so stunned that it was a matter of almost no moment when the stopping mechanism of the bathtub did not work, so that she had to settle for a shower instead of a sleepy soak, or when, presently, her bedside light did not function either; all this in spite of the imposing trappings.

Jenny, necessarily reduced to the hotel's brochure about what to see in Juarez, offered to turn off her own lamp at once, but Mary assured her, "Not on my account." Unlike many people, she found a faint reflected glow on her eyelids a positive aid to sleep, a pleasant borderland between wakefulness and dreaming. Back turned to the other bed, she gazed between dropping lashes at the door in its well of dimness beyond the bathroom and facing closet . . .

. . . And heard herself arguing away the marriage to Spencer Hume. She had been mainly a devil's advocate at first, because neither of them regarded such a step lightly, but little by little, like a convert to vegetarianism putting someone else off his chosen food, she had convinced them both, although at the end Spence had said, between bewilderment and anger, "Damn it, Mary, we can't *both* have been crazy."

Unlike people in plays and books and possibly real life, they had not remained friends. They had avoided each other assiduously, not easy in Santa Fe and posing difficulties for hostesses who had entertained them both, until Spence's company had offered to transfer him to San Francisco and he had leaped at the chance. Taking with him his blue gaze which could suddenly fall into a reverie about the oddest things, and the flicker of beginning gray in the dark hair above his ears although he was only thirty-four.

But that wasn't Spence. That was . . .

"Mary," Jenny was saying in a frightened, insistent voice. "There's someone at the door, trying to get in."

Mary, jerked out of her dark-gold, sleep-buzzing trance, saw that the doorknob was indeed turning, sprang out of bed, cried distractedly, "Oh, I don't believe this!" for the benefit of whoever it was, and fumbled her way into her robe as she went to the door. "Who is it?"

"Alfredo."

At close to eleven o'clock, if not after? Still a little dazed, Mary undid the chain which was more of a decoration than any real safeguard and opened the door a cautious two inches. A pile of recognizable books met her eye, with above them the expression-

66

less face of the bellboy. There was no apology for the late hour, no query, even by means of facial gymnastics, as to whether he had disturbed them.

Mary opened the door wider, took the books, thanked him, didn't ask where he had found them, and knew that she was spineless to give him a dollar for this eccentric and semihostile delivery. It crossed her mind as she closed the door after him that possibly he made a lucrative practice of holding odd items for ransom—in the flurry of arrival people were apt to put down things like cameras or prescription sunglasses—but perhaps she was prejudiced because of that signal down the corridor.

"This place is crazy," said Jenny with conviction from her bed. "Doesn't anybody ever knock?"

"Apparently not. Well, let's hope that's the last of it." Mary went back to the door and hung the "Do Not Disturb" sign on the outer knob; it was a small deterrent but it might help. She returned to her bed, half-expecting it to buckle to the floor, exchanged a last farewell with Jenny, who turned off her lamp, and tried to recapture her earlier drowsiness without, however, resorting to Spence.

She kept an eye on the doorknob for a while, in case the staff should suddenly remember more errands here, but it began to swim away as fatigue took over. There was a dim and reassuring wash of gold in that corner of the room; evidently the rambling circuit of the Casa de Flores stayed lit through the night. In the other bed, Jenny gave a few settling flounces and retreated almost at once into a sleep-bound silence.

Mary fell asleep herself, her consciousness grazed

now and then by the sounds of people calling to each other in the corridor outside, and once, although that might have been part of a dream, a muted cry.

In another motel room, less than a mile away, a girl who looked extraordinarily pretty even with her hair in rollers was saying to a man's shadow projected on the wall opposite the open door of the bathroom, "I declare, if I'd known you were going to keep me locked up like this I wouldn't have come."

"You weren't locked up, and I told you tonight was business."

Someone warier might have taken alarm from his tone; the girl did not. "Well, what about tomorrow? Is that business too?" Because she was creaming her face as she spoke, and then turning her head a little to examine one perfect eyebrow, she missed the lifting and down-chopping motion of the shadow arm, a soundless expression of rage.

But the voice that came out of the bathroom a second later was calm. "Tomorrow we'll do whatever you like. After—" he had had time to take her measure, and he was almost playful, like a man holding candy just out of a child's reach"—you do something for me."

7

Mary, waking to the unfamiliar walls and furniture and window, thought at first that the day was overcast. It took her moments to remember that a certain hour of the morning here the sunlight was so white that the very air seemed to fume with it, turning the bluest of skies smoky by contrast.

Jenny's bed was empty, and the familiar worry sprang up, to be coped with by the familiar arguments. She had gone for an early swim—but the watch on the night table said that it wasn't early, a little after nine-thirty, and when Mary went into the bathroom Jenny's bathing-suit was hanging from the shower rail.

She's a big girl now, thought Mary, and had scarcely completed this far-from-comforting reflection when there was a tap and then the sound of the key and Jenny came in, triumphantly bearing a newspaper. "I got the last one. You were sleeping so soundly that I didn't want to wake you."

She wanted the Jumble, of course, because events in El Paso could scarcely be of interest. Although— Mary finished dressing—Jenny also entertained herself with the unlikely conjunction of names in wedding announcements, for which she had an eagle eye. ("Miss Ethel Racey and Frederick Scoot . . . maid of honor, Miss Glenda Walker.")

At this hour of the morning, the dining room was being readied for lunch. The coffee shop, sparsely populated, appeared to be in the grip of one of the internecine wars which occasionally occur in public places, the hostess in rivetted conversation with the cashier, waitresses in dissolving and regrouping knots, busboys, of insufficient rank for these councils, staring enviously. Factions in the kitchen, thought Mary, or a key employee threatening to quit and sides being taken.

She was eventually able to order orange juice, cantaloupe, and coffee, recommending the fruit to Jenny, who shook her head and wanted only a small glass of tomato juice and coffee into which she would unobtrusively drop a saccharine tablet. "Suit yourself," said Mary, careless, "but I thought you might like to have a look at the shops this morning, with an eye to birthday presents or even Christmas, and it's apt to be a lengthy process."

This wasn't true—to the disappointment of neophytes who looked forward to some keen haggling, shopping in this part of the city was a straightforward, one-price affair—but to Mary's gratification Jenny succumbed to the melon. A waitress presently tore herself away from the far wall to refill their

70

coffee cups, but was still so fascinated by the murmurs and gesticulations going on at the cashier's stand that she kept the urn tilted and Mary, instinctively following her gaze, was caught unaware by a hot flow out of the saucer, over the table edge, and into her lap.

The ensuing fluster with a hastily produced damp napkin seemed to communicate itself around the room. Mary reassured the girl, who looked panicky under the menacing regard of the hostess, and let a negligent interval go by before she said to Jenny, "There is nothing quite like cold coffee, inside *or* outside," and left the table.

In the upstairs corridor, icy in her wet dress and pastily clinging slip, she took automatic note of the room service cart outside the room which was beginning to assume a Poelike character, and the cleaning cart, midway along the other side. A maid—her back was to the light from the window at the end of the corridor, but from her height and the outline of her head she was the earring-hunter of yesterday—was bundling linen into a laundry bag while she listened to the man who was already so strangely familiar to Mary that she could have picked him out of a crowded station.

The man from the pool, concerned about Jenny. Mary let herself into her room just as he was starting to turn.

She had travelled light to Juarez as always, two dresses for daytime and two for night, so it was a matter of the mint-leafed white which she had worn in the car on the way down. Fortunately, it was of a fabric which started to shed wrinkles the moment it was placed on a hanger. Mary washed her coffee-stained clothes rapidly and, key in hand, stood at the door for a puzzled moment, as if there were something else she should be doing before she left the room.

It couldn't, said the age-old and totally false reassurance in such instances, be very important.

On the half-landing between the slippery flights of stairs, she encountered the man from the pool, who had been openly waiting for her. He wasn't the astonishment of the night before, but she still felt a small jolt along her nerves—because so often she had exited from after-theater ladies' rooms to where Spence waited, or come home to find him pacing her living room when she had been delayed at work?

He was friendly and casual, and said by way of explanation that he had realized only after leaving her last night that he hadn't introduced himself—Owen St. Ives. He knew Mary's name, from Jenny. He added that he had been trying to find out from the maid, without success, the identity of the invisible occupants at the end of the corridor. "None of my business, but I'm torn between a case of plague and somebody who's been getting white roses from the Mafia. Unfortunately, the maid doesn't speak English."

He glanced inquiringly at Mary as he spoke, as though she might have succeeded where he had failed. His eyes weren't brown, as they had looked in the orange glow from the wall sconces the night before, but very dark blue. "I know," began Mary, and stopped, because it would be ridiculous to confide to a man she didn't even know the woman's strange and

72

silent invasion of her room.

They had reached the doorway of the coffee shop, and Owen St. Ives lifted a hand in greeting to Jenny, still at the table. He said to Mary, "You're staying at least through tonight, aren't you? Then I'll see you both later, I hope."

Mary rejoined her cousin, and saw that her impression from a distance had been correct: Jenny wore the faint remains of a blush. Clearly she had a penchant for men considerably older than herself, and just as clearly Brian Beardsley had been supplanted.

Good, said Mary to herself with force, because this meant that the problem had largely evaporated. Still, it was something of a surprise to realize that her senses might have betrayed her again, there on the stairs; that St. Ives, who could have registered only a blur of motion as she entered her room, might very well have been waiting not for her, but for Jenny.

Out into the blaze of light to the car which, presently, Mary surrendered to the watchful eye of a brown-uniformed policeman. Even without a parking meter to be fed by him, this was standard procedure. Where no such official existed, bands of small boys took over.

In various shops—the main market could wait until afternoon—she and Jenny looked at tooled leather handbags, flower-decorated straw bags, onyx chess sets and pottery owls, sheaves of brilliant paper flowers, hand-embroidered cotton blouses and dresses, mirrors set in sunbursts of tin or mosaics of rainbow glass. Under this assault of color and variety Jenny began to acquire a glazed and indecisive ex-

73

pression, but finally bought a mantilla for her mother and a pair of silver filigree earrings which were not, Mary considered, going to do a thing for Gerald Acton.

Having completed the last purchase, Jenny roamed off to another counter, came back, said, "This is so old hat to you that you must be tired of it, Mary. Why don't you wait for me a few minutes in the car?"

Mary thought she knew the reason for this suggestion. She said, "Jenny, if you were thinking of buying anything for me—" and was interrupted by one of the rare, teasing smiles and, "Don't I have any rights around here?"

She started obediently off for the car, a figure at once cool and vivid in the simple leaf-patterned dress, and was stopped almost at once by a hailing "Mary Vaughan" from Daniel Brennan. It was a peculiar form of address, much more recognizing than the use of just her first name, which Southwesterners employed instantly, or a formal greeting. He walked to her car with her, so unalarming that she was amazed at her own suspicions the evening before, and explained that he was in search of a decent light bulb for his reading lamp; the one in place was so dim that moths flew away from it.

"Mine doesn't work at all, thank you for reminding me," said Mary, and, after a further comment on the boil of black-tinged clouds which she hadn't noticed until then beginning to build up in the west, was handed into her car. She got out again almost at once, tipped the policeman to whom this courtesy belonged, was sealed gallantly in once more, wound down the window for a stir of air, idly picked up the newspaper which Jenny had carried away from the breakfast table.

Or not quite idly, because without conscious thought she looked at the index for the weather, turned to the proper page, saw that there would be no point in any further long-distance telephone calls. Both New York and Boston were sunny, with temperatures in the seventies, so the Actons were undoubtedly in Wellfleet.

Although that seemed academic now.

At the motel, it was clear that Jenny was not going to practice any turns for the time being. The name-tagged group was there in force, tossing a beach ball back and forth, full of carried-over merriment from the night before: one of their number had only to call loudly, "Zap!" to elicit a general chorus of laughter and some shoulder-punching among the men.

Jenny tried to stare them into a tighter group, standing on the deck and spinning her cap on her forefinger. Mary, more determined if less militant, slid over the side and managed to preempt a lane at the very edge. Her head came up in mid-stroke at the sound of a sharp scream when she was halfway down the pool, but it was only a woman who had had a toe playfully bitten by one of the men.

Screaming in the water broke a basic rule of conduct, but apart from Jenny's severe gaze it provoked no reaction at all; a waiter passing by with a tray of drinks didn't even glance over his shoulder. Frolicking here was evidently done in full cry. Mary wondered what would happen to a swimmer in real trouble, figured out the answer without much difficulty, and saw presently that Jenny had sat down and was no longer glowering. She was looking up at Owen St. Ives, who said something to her and then pulled out a chair and joined her.

Mary had been going to abandon the pool until it was less crowded, but she did six more laps in the clear, crisp-feeling water so that Jenny should not see her in the role of chaperone again. She wondered about her cousin and Owen St. Ives as she swam. There were men who found youth a challenge for its own sake, but he did not look like one of them. Was he simply being—awkward word, it sounded some-how connected with warts—avuncular? Was he here on vacation, and tiring of his own company?

The ball in play hit her on the head with a sur-prising thump, and a man cried jovially, "Hey, sorry about that!" Just don't bite my toe, thought Mary, and swam cautiously past him and climbed out. Owen St. Ives got to his feet as she ap-proached the table, but with no intention of leav-ing. He looked mildly pleased with himself. "I was just telling Jenny—"

A waiter arrived with a tray holding iced tea and two golden Bacardis on the rocks. There was even a glass of water for Mary, who diluted her drinks some-what. This sure choice shook her until she realized that he would have asked Jenny what to order.

The waiter went away. "I've unravelled part of the mystery upstairs," said St. Ives, "but we're all sworn to secrecy so the room-service waiter I talked to won't lose his job. What we have there is an Ameri-can with a nervous breakdown and a male nurse. He must be readily recognizable, because he's paying

76

heavily not to be seen."

"But there's nothing disgraceful about a nervous breakdown," said Mary involuntarily.

"Certainly not, but there are times when you'd just as soon not have one made public. If you were running for reelection after a questionable voting record, say, or had a proxy fight on your hands, or were in the middle of a divorce and wanted custody of a child or children . . ." St. Ives shrugged, letting that tail off as though he had scarcely embarked upon a list of possible motives.

Mary could not have said why there was something unspoken in the air: the suggestion that other and less harmless states of mind could be presented as nervous breakdowns. But even the bizarrely run Casa de Flores wouldn't harbor a dangerous psychotic.

(Although if he had arrived looking only like a man badly in need of complete rest and quiet, how would they know?)

The air darkened suddenly as the morning's massed clouds moved over the sun, the now-deserted swimming pool grew a gooseflesh frill, a new sharp wind blew Mary's bathing-cap off the table. Owen St. Ives glanced at the sky. "Going to pour," he said, and then, casually, as he retrieved her cap and pocketed his cigarettes, "Did you happen to hear anything from that direction during the night?"

Jenny shook her head at once and said, "Not I." Mary remembered the half-dreamed sound like an aborted cry, and the peculiar atmosphere in the coffee shop at breakfast as though the staff buzzed with something. But if Jenny had been so inordinately frightened of the chambermaid, how would she react to this? "Neither did I," said Mary firmly.

She glanced at her cousin as she spoke, and saw with surprise that she needn't have worried; Jenny was gazing at St. Ives with only interest and speculation. The close proximity of a man with nervous problems severe enough to warrant the presence of a nurse didn't seem to bother her at all. So her source of alarm, first showing itself in tension at the sound of the telephone in Santa Fe the night before they left, was, unlikely though it seemed, a woman.

A slender woman with cropped dark hair, Mary amended, because just for a second the maid must have looked to Jenny like someone else. Encountered where?

It couldn't matter; Jenny had recovered at once and seemed to have forgotten the incident. She said as they reached the archway just ahead of the first drops of rain, "Those people in the pool were going to a bullfight."

It was clear from her dubious tone that in spite of her extreme squeamishness at the sight of blood she was beginning to wonder if this event was something she would regret having missed, later on. Mary was not anxious to repeat her own single experience. She could not endorse the prim outrage of the woman sitting next to her, who had said with conviction, "They would never allow this in St. Louis," but neither did she care for the streams of crimson coursing down the massive shoulders where the banderillas had been planted at the outset. No matter what Hemingway said, it seemed an odd way for a bull to express his thorough enjoyment of the sport.

Still, she said, "Would you like me to see if I can get tickets? They might have them right here."

Jenny hesitated. "Is there an awful lot of gore?"

"Well, the bull doesn't die of fright," said Mary reasonably, and Jenny gave a little shudder and shook her head. "Forget I mentioned it."

The interchange was so normal, and so unrelated to what had gone before, that Mary's mind had already dismissed that puzzling moment of real fear. It gave her nothing whatever in the way of warning.

8

It was at lunch that the first invisible move was made.

Owen St. Ives had been accurate in his weather prediction. A hard gray rain was beating down on the flowers and lawns and bouncing up from the walks, with the result that the dining room was crowded with guests who would otherwise have ventured out elsewhere. With the exception of St. Ives, all the people even vaguely familiar to Mary were there: the Indian woman, in a sari of burnt-orange as slumbrous as a fire just getting under way; the conventioneers, giving complicated drink orders ("No, hold that, I'll have a margharita instead of a daiquiri, but forget the salt") to a patient waiter; Daniel Brennan, alone at a table for two, gazing expectantly at the dining room entrance and, occasionally, his watch.

Jenny, who evidently regarded her breakfast melon as an entering wedge in every respect, wanted only a cup of soup until Mary said with dangerous amiability, "Why don't you just have a crust of bread and a sip of water instead? Then I'll really look like a villain."

It was the first time she had brought the issue so squarely into the open—and, from her startled and then narrowed gaze, the first time Jenny had contemplated herself in this light. She obviously didn't mind and perhaps even enjoyed the glances drawn by her pipe-cleaner construction; to be thought of as being punished was a different matter. With dignity, she ordered a chicken sandwich.

That didn't mean she would do more than taste it, Mary warned herself, but it seemed to her that the starvation pattern was beginning to break down under the pressure of a strange place and a new face. When the sandwich arrived, accompanied by her own shrimp salad, Jenny opened it briskly, scraped off all the butter, added salt and pepper, and took a purposeful bite. She was thoroughly aware of what was going on; she said ironically to Mary, "Eat it, dear, it's broccoli . . . actually, it's not bad."

From its very force—the dining room windows were now tall wavering greenish blurs enclosed in gold-and-brown print—the rain couldn't last much longer. Jenny said yes to Mary's question as to whether she would like to visit the market later (kept talking, she might absentmindedly consume a few of the tostados thrust invitingly into her guacamole salad) but her attention was clearly elsewhere. She smiled suddenly, lifted a hand in greeting, said across the table, "That's a girl I met in my mad dash for the paper this morning. She seems quite nice as well as gorgeous, which I don't think is fair."

But gorgeous was an overblown adjective for the girl whom Mary glanced at presently, and beautiful or striking didn't apply either. She was overwhelmingly, enchantingly pretty, with an air of being on the edge of some delightful adventure even while sitting still: there was a suggestion of breath caught, lips about to curve and part. It wasn't only a matter of coloring, which was shades of honey; it was millimeters off the norm—a very faint tilt to her nose, a very faint almonding of her eyes, which placed her in a special category. Like a rose in exactly the right stage of bloom, she was a pleasure to behold.

She had been seated at a table for four. She lifted her face to a waiter and indicated that there would be other people coming, and in spite of all that heavy artillery she looked shy and apologetic. The waiter departed as a man off to the crusades and returned almost at once with a daiquiri, although a couple at the neighboring table were still stranded with only silver, napkins, and ice water.

"She looks almost edible," said Mary with sincerity. "From California, I'll bet. They seem to have a monopoly."

Jenny shook her head. "She has a Southern accent." There wasn't a trace of envy in her voice, only pride at being on even a nodding acquaintance with such a ravishing creature, and Mary gazed at her with sudden affection. She could be maddening at times, but mixed in with the perversity and stubbornness there was a very sound and sturdy streak.

The rain stopped with faucet abruptness, the last drops falling through sunlight. There was an instant stir throughout the dining room as people who had been lingering over coffee began to shift in their chairs, gather handbags, crane in search of waiters. Mary's roving glance noted that Daniel Brennan's business colleague had never turned up and he was now lunching alone. Reminded of their brief exchange that morning, she went to the desk when the check had been settled, waited through a flurry of people checking out, informed the clerk about her nonfunctioning bedside lamp.

It was the difficult one, but today he made no pretense of not being able to understand Mary; indeed, as though to add to her stock of Spanish should she care to return to it, he said, "Ah, lampara." Patronizingly, he became all teeth. "I will see that the maid bring a new bulb."

"But it isn't the bulb," said Mary, spurred to give him a steady smile back. "I've already tried that. It's the lamp itself."

This "Ah!" had the alertness of a surgeon's, finding a malignancy, and the clerk made a note, with flourishes. It seemed somehow too easy. "And did you receive your libros? Your books?"

If not war, this was certainly a skirmish. "Yes, thank you," said Mary. "It was well worth being waked up for." She turned away and saw Jenny, who had drifted to the postcard display at the end of the counter, in conversation with the remarkable girl from the dining room.

She was small—Jenny seemed to tower over her— and Mary guessed her to be about twenty-two. A fashion magazine would have wanted her to lose at least five pounds, but that would have been like wanting a slender apricot or a hollow-cheeked peach. Up close, her warmly tanned skin was silky, her eyes a melting gray-green. In accordance with the habit of the day, Jenny introduced her as Astrid and asked Mary if they could give her a lift into town; through a misunderstanding, the aunt and uncle she was with had gone off without her.

"I'm a tiny bit nervous about taking a taxi here," said Astrid abashedly, "but if it's a bother—"

If she had been less disarming, Mary could have imagined whole processions of women arranging to leave her behind. As it was, she seemed to present no more of a threat than baby powder, although there was nothing in the least babyish about her. Here, something twitched at the edge of Mary's mind and as abruptly let go. "No bother at all," she said, smiling at the girl. "We were going to the market anyway, so whenever you're ready . . ."

This proved to be at once, not surprisingly; Astrid had obviously cut her lunch short, when she realized her predicament, in the hope of a ride with someone she had at least met. In the car, she asked to be dropped off at any place convenient for Mary near the optician's on the main street where her aunt and uncle were having eyeglass prescriptions filled; she would meet them there after she did some souvenir-shopping.

Astrid lived in North Carolina (this in answer to a question from Jenny) and this was her first visit to the Southwest. No, she had never been to New York, but had heard that it was *expensive*. After a time, Mary stopped listening to compared notes and gave her whole attention to the traffic. Driving habits in Juarez had improved in the last few years, and taxis no longer looked like discarded frozen-food containers, but it was still necessary to be on the alert for boys darting fearlessly between cars with cartons of duty-free cigarettes for sale, or wobbling alongside on bicycles and offering themselves as guides.

Astrid got out at the appointed corner, expressing thanks and the hope that if her aunt and uncle didn't decide to start the return journey to Albuquerque that afternoon she would see them later. Mary was struck by the frequency with which, in less than twenty-four hours, she had heard these words from people encountered for the first time. She glanced back automatically as she completed her turn into the parking area for the market, but Astrid had vanished.

. . . For a moment, standing close to Mary Vaughan —fair hair looking lamplit, hazel eyes clear and unmarked in a face not dark with a rain of blood but only touched lightly by the sun—he had nearly seized her throat then and there and to hell with the consequences. His heart had raced with the raging impulse, his brain ached with it.

He had smiled at her instead, although it was increasingly difficult, now that she was within actual, physical reach, to remind himself that she had to know why she was dying. There would be no point in dispatching her with almost the speed of a sniper —but he promised himself that she would pay him back for every second of this charade, which was forcing him to take more tranquilizers than his prescription called for.

She had glanced at him peculiarly once or twice,

as if searching for another identity behind his features, but she couldn't be really suspicious because she was still here with the stick-figure girl, Jenny. If he had had any hatred to spare he would have applied it in that direction, because she had to be detached long enough for a fatal accident to befall Mary Vaughan—if not in the pool, on the almost glassy stairs—and she stuck like a burr.

The Casa de Flores must have a discreet doctor to summon in emergencies, and he felt sure that accident, in the case of a U.S. citizen staying at a tourist-oriented Mexican motel, would be a verdict welcome in all quarters.

Meanwhile, there was an essential call to make, and instinct took him back over the border to El Paso and the first telephone booth he could find. He was in luck; it was his sister who answered the direct-dialling and asked, after her first anxious inquiry, "Where are you?"

Unhesitatingly, he named a town fifty miles to the north of Santa Fe, where he and his wife had had a primitive cabin for vacations and an occasional long weekend of fishing, hiking, brief dips in an icy stream. Where, if she had not done so much internal bleeding after she was turned away from Mary Vaughan's door, his wife would have been able to heal all her wounds. In his mind he struck down again, furiously, the doctor's assertion that the mortal damage had already been done by that time. Those were the tales they told children.

". . . the *cabin?*" Eunice Howe was asking incredulously, and he scratched the edge of a coin gently over the mouthpiece and said, " . . . friends. I can't hear you very well, can you hear me? How is everything there?"

Everything being the funeral arrangements, about which he cared nothing at all, and the investigation in progress, in which his interest was vital. People taken to emergency rooms passed through a number of hands. Was it possible that the police had somehow learned of Mary Vaughan's involvement, tried to question her, discovered her hasty departure, linked it with his own if they knew about that?

He gripped the receiver, staring at the pebbled wall of the phone booth, and heard his sister say that the police had arrested a boy with a previous record but were still searching for the weapon. " . . . And I hope you'll approve of what we've arranged with Homan's, the—well, you know. When will you be back?"

"Tomorrow," he said, setting a seal on Mary Vaughan. "I don't know what time, but tomorrow."

"What does pobrecita mean?" asked Jenny.

Poor little thing. Mary replying falsely that she didn't know, had also heard it murmured behind them more than once in their jostled progress through the narrow aisles of the market, all converging on the central area with its heaped bins of vivid, outsize fruits and vegetables.

The diminutive would have seemed odd to apply to tall Jenny if simple alarm at this teeming place with its lively vendors and overspill of brooms, straw hats, puppets, salad bowls, bull horns, handbags—just in one short distance—hadn't given her the appearance of a defensive child. She pretended not to hear

87

the incessant coaxings to look, to buy, so that the stall-keepers pursued her the more assiduously. When Mary said, "No, gracias," they desisted at once, and that was when the "pobrecita" followed, as though she were in the habit of denying the poor little thing decent sustenance as well.

Gradually, at the sight of other tourists bargaining over carved wooden masks and painted pottery jars as they stepped casually around spilled liquid or trodden lettuce leaves on the uneven concrete floor, Jenny recovered her composure and even a trace of adventure. How much, she inquired of Mary, would one of those curly black iron candlesticks be?

"About two dollars, or two-fifty. Why don't you ask?"

Jenny did. She had evidently been keeping an ear cocked, because at the two-fifty price she shook her head and said with a firm and practiced air, "Too much."

"Too much!" Mary recognized this zestful man from the year before, and it was mutual; he dropped an eyelid at her in the midst of dealing with Jenny. From nowhere, like lightning, he produced a candle and thrust it into one of the two holders. "How beautiful, yes? You are never without light. *Too much?* You are rich Yankee, and I—" he allowed his curly dark head to loll dramatically toward his chest"—am poor man. Big family. Sixteen kids."

The wrought iron was graceful, like all Mexican work, and Jenny was no match for this seasoned mixture of drollery and reproach. She bought the candlestick, the candle having been whisked thriftily out of it, and watched it wrapped in the ubiquitous newspaper by a fleet little boy who had also appeared where he wasn't before. She muttered deflatedly as the man went to another stall for change, "I suppose that's the oldest of the sixteen."

It wasn't an observation which required an answer —and, Mary realized a second too late, Jenny wouldn't have heard one in any case. She had turned her head, seeking the source of a sudden gay burst of mariachi music, and all at once she was as stiff and deaf and dumb as a statue.

Mary followed her gaze, saw only tourists, the back of one of the musicians, the sunny street outside the market entrance. The two men they had passed on their way in still sat at a sidewalk table, lingering over cans of beer and squeezed limes. With a small acceleration of her heartbeat, because they were at the edge of a confrontation, she said directly, "Who was that, Jenny?"

If it were possible for stone eyes to liquefy and achieve color, they would have bent exactly Jenny's glance. "Who was what?"

And unspokenly, as a week's cautious cameraderie was wiped out in a matter of seconds, What business is it of yours? It mightn't be unusual at eighteen to consider that you had passed the point of having to answer to anyone—but Mary thought of the Actons' very real worry and her own sense of responsibility, and felt a flash of anger at being put in the position of a prying stranger. A passerby bumped into her and apologized, but her eyes held Jenny's without flickering. "You seem to have seen someone who startled you," she said levelly.

But the moment got away from her, if it had ever

been there. The jaunty stall-keeper returned with change and smiles and flourishes, and Jenny had had time to recover her wits. "That woman in red over there," she said. "It's a Siamese cat she's holding, but wouldn't you swear it was a monkey?"

Yes, if you looked at it with your eyes shut, thought Mary. It was clearly time, more than time, to stop pretending that there was no issue at stake. She said calmly, driving down a feeling that, like a member of some Satanist cult, she was about to utter a name which should only be pronounced while standing inside protective lines of chalk, "Was it by any chance Brian Beardsley?"

9

If Jenny had not kept up an uncharacteristic flow of small talk all the way back to the motel, Mary might have convinced herself that she had imagined that instant of focused stillness in the market. She had taken what she considered a decisive plunge, and braced herself for she wasn't sure what, and she could have gotten just as much drama out of, "Was it Christopher Robin?"

Because, far from any guilty starts or stage astonishment, Jenny had simply drawn her dark brows together, narrowed her formidable eyelashes a little, and said with a puzzled air, "*Brian?* What would he be doing in Mexico?"

The temptation to vindicate herself—"You'd have to ask your friend Myrna about that, because she's the one who talked to him last"—was strong, but Mary veered instinctively away from that course. She knew that what she had elicited wasn't an answer,

91

and in fact might have been a schoolgirl's parry to avoid a direct lie, but she was shaken. How likely was it, really, that Beardsley had found out about a decision made only the night before they left Santa Fe? Jenny certainly hadn't made or received any telephone calls, and neither of Mary's neighbors knew about the trip. And the thought of Beardsley mounting a watch somewhere with binoculars was completely ridiculous.

There was the blue car which had followed them for most of the way, but Mary had had time for a glance as they passed it with its hood up and it wasn't new enough to be a rental, surely the only transportation for a man arriving by plane. Jenny had been living with him, had precipitated a family crisis because of him, would certainly have recognized him even in silhouette behind a steering-wheel—and it was she who had called Mary's attention to the car.

On the other hand, she had undeniably seen someone (or, thought Mary for the first time, a conjunction of someones) who had astonished and upset her. She had developed an instant longing for a stop to buy facial tissues and emery boards, thereby changing the subject with swiftness, and she had chattered in the supermarket. How funny to see people doing their shopping while sipping at a can of cold beer. Wasn't it peculiar in such a beer-drinking country that there wasn't a pretzel to be found? Why didn't the magazine racks contain a Spanish-English dictionary?

And so on, until Mary began to develop a slight headache. Who had her cousin met in Juarez? Owen St. Ives, swimming coach, she thought, surprised at her own edge. Delectable Astrid. Daniel Brennan, in whose company Jenny had spent perhaps thirty seconds, could scarcely be said to count.

The clerk had an air of importance as he handed over the room key and then reached behind him. "Una carta," he said, enjoying his game with Mary, "por la senorita Acton."

Jenny looked bewildered. She accepted the envelope, which Mary saw addressed in a bold blue hand, opened it, unfolded a single sheet of notepaper which she dropped into her bag after reading the brief contents. "Astrid," she said to Mary. "They're checking out this afternoon but she wants to thank us for the ride. Shall we go on up? I'm dying to get into the pool."

The aunt and uncle were thrifty and negligent by turns, then; they drove all the way to Juarez to have their eyeglass prescriptions filled at cut-rate prices, but threw away a day's tariff because check-out time was one o'clock. Astrid must belong to the head-of-a-pin school of handwriting, Mary reflected idly, because her explanation and gratitude had been compressed into a single line.

The door at the end of the corridor stayed closed as she and Jenny approached their room; presumably the occupants were now familiar with their footsteps. For some reason it was a chilling little thought. Inside, Mary pressed the switch of her bedside lamp and was not surprised that it still didn't work. She ought to have mentioned the bathtub stopper, so that that wouldn't get fixed either. She said when Jenny emerged in bathing-suit and robe, "Why don't you go on down, while I have another try at getting this thing repaired?"

But, as with Alfredo and the books, she didn't pursue the matter of the lamp. She had made reservations here only through tonight, and although it might be possible to extend them, or move to another motel, it seemed important first to know whether or not Brian Beardsley had come looking for Jenny.

The Taylor house, close to the road with a circular drive, was the logical place for a visitor to inquire, as the Ulibarris' was set a hundred yards back and they harbored Doberman pinschers behind a chain-link fence. After a considerable delay, because she didn't know the first name and the telephone book was apparently rife with Taylors, Mary listened as the distant ringing began.

"That's the phone," said Pippa Taylor alertly as Meg started the car. Although apparently deaf to the sound of her sister washing the dishes with an exasperated crash, or pushing the furniture screechingly around in preparation for vacuuming, she never missed this signal. Now, she undid her seat-belt. "Quick, give me your key."

"Let it go, we're late now, thanks to you taking an hour over your face."

But Pippa was aready out of the car, extending her hand imperatively. "I *can't* let it go, it might be Becky about my sleeping-bag. Or," she said, fast and inspired, "it might be Mom, telling us not to come now because she's going to have therapy or something."

Mrs. Taylor had in fact called three days ago with

94

just such a message, and Meg produced the key. "Well, hurry up. I'll give you exactly one minute, and then, I warn you, I'm taking off without you."

Pippa raced back to the front door, her gait at odds with the blusher and eye-shadow carefully applied because you never knew who you might meet in the course of visiting your mother in the hospital; the place was crawling with internes. She had to struggle with the key, because it was very slightly bent, but the telephone went on ringing as if with a promise to wait.

It did wait, until the second before Pippa snatched up the receiver and said a breathless "Hello?" to a dial tone.

A mile away, the grounds of the Romero house had been searched for the knife without which the police had no case at all. The grounds weren't extensive, and it didn't take long to determine that there had been no fresh digging. A rickety structure at the back of the property contained only six outraged chickens and an innocent bag of feed. The leveling of a compost heap turned up nothing more interesting than a well-rotted dog collar.

Still, it was the gloomy conviction of Gil Candelaria, the investigating officer in charge, that unless the field of search were confined to a sheet of plate glass it was next to impossible to say with certainty that a smallish object wasn't in a given locality—and Leroy Romero seemed confident and even a little mocking.

Which, Candelaria conceded to himself, he had every right to be thus far. On the evening in question, he claimed to have been cruising with friends, a favorite after-dark activity among his age group although it was a continuing marvel to the police that they could afford the gas. If the friends went on supporting his story—as they undoubtedly would; in spite of his youth and slender build, Romero shimmered with menace like a radiator with heat waves —the police couldn't prove otherwise. The presence of his wallet in the dead woman's driveway could be explained away in seconds: the thief and real attacker had dropped it there.

He had at first denied ownership of a knife at all, and when a passing detective had asked sarcastically, "What'd you stab that guy from Phoenix with, a sharp spoon?" he had continued glibly ". . . since then." Confronted with his informing friend's statement about a knife which was a prized possession, he had looked openly deadly for a moment and then said he had lost it a month ago.

Where had he lost it? On a camping trip in the Pecos Wilderness. There was some derisive laughter at this, because he was patently as interested in camping as a snake in a shoe sale, but again they couldn't shake him. Nor had they been able to locate anyone in the area who had seen or heard the victim before the pick-up driver had stopped for her.

Candelaria, a man twice Leroy Romero's size and age, shut his eyes and tried to put himself in the boy's position. He had attacked a woman and she had gotten away from him (because—they thought they had this figured out—a coronary unit had been in the neighborhood, its siren sounding like a police car's). He would have a wild vision of the woman giving the police a usable description of him. He would know that there must be blood on him, so it would be a matter of bolting home to wash himself and his clothing.

He hadn't worn gloves—the bite mark on his thumb suggested that—so, apart from being his pride and his status symbol, the knife bore his fingerprints as well as the woman's blood. Where to conceal it in the dark between her driveway and his own, safe from searchers but findable when this blew over?

Much better to keep it with him, thought Candelaria, now warming thoroughly to his theme. There was an outside faucet beside the Romero back steps, where he could wash the knife and then hide it—where?

That convenient faucet (sluice his face and hands at the same time?) kept bobbing up in Candelaria's mind. Because it suggested something else, so familiar to him from boyhood that he hadn't given it the attention an alert and curious outsider might? He did now, concentrating on the suspect's back yard, trying to recapture a half-forgotten formula, thinking about weather conditions at the time involved.

He hadn't yet received a copy of the detailed autopsy report, but a glance at his watch showed him that he might still catch the police surgeon; Stoddard was a man to avoid calling at home if at all possible. He pulled the telephone toward him, consulted the list of numbers pasted on a pull-out board of his desk, and dialled.

Mary had just said goodbye to a bewildered Mrs. Ulibarri, over a distant chorus of background barking, when the light tap sounded at her door.

She hadn't put the chain on, but at least the knob wasn't turning. Jenny always signalled, so was this, incredibly, a maintenance man about her lamp? The chambermaid, having thought of a new place to look for the earring? No, she would have come right in. Mary called a query, and opened the door to Owen St. Ives.

For a moment, she was terrified. Something had happened to Jenny at the pool, even though in the water she was like a bird in its element, and he had come to break it to her. Then he said, "I have a great favor to ask of you, if you're not busy for the next fifteen minutes or so. I've been—"

He broke off there, studying her with the blue gaze that was so much darker than Spence's. He asked curiously, "Do I frighten you for some reason? At times—I notice because you have very pretty eyes, you look as if . . ."

"No, of course not," said Mary, feeling the blood rise to her face. "It's just that you remind me of someone I used to know." To her own ears that sounded very equivocal, and she stepped back at once, turned to the desk for a cigarette to give her something to do with her hands, took time to inspect it because this was the kind of moment in which she might well light the filter end. "If it's something I can do?"

"I've been entrusted with twenty-five dollars to buy a birthday present for my sister-in-law, preferably a poncho or a shawl. I don't know why my brother would think me capable of this, as I'm no good about women's clothes, but she wants something from Mexico," said St. Ives, "and I wondered if you'd help me pick something out."

Mary was obscurely glad about part of his statement; if necessary, Spence could have selected an entire wardrobe for a woman without going wrong anywhere. She said doubtfully, "Oh, but—"

"She's tall," said St. Ives, recognizing this demur, "and . . . large. She has red hair." He considered for a few seconds. "Very red," he added.

Mary thought privately that anyone tall and large with very red hair would be better off without a poncho, but she said, "Well, I'll try, if you can give me five minutes first."

He nodded his appreciation. "I'll get the car and meet you in front. We'll be quick about this, I promise."

Mary washed her face rapidly, put on light fresh makeup, combed her hair. Her dress was beginning to feel like a uniform, but the one that had been splashed with coffee wasn't quite dry and in any case, after that remark about her eyes, she was going to be every inch a gift counsellor.

Owen St. Ives wasn't in front, because a number of guests were arriving to fill the vacuum left by the after-lunch exodus. Mary caught his signalling wave and threaded her way to the other side of the cobbled court. She was in the car, and it was moving, before she realized with astonishment that for the first time in almost forty-eight hours she had completely forgotten that she was not alone here. She said, "Oh, wait a minute, I've got to let Jenny know that I'm going."

He didn't hear her; he had his head out the win-

99

dow, backing clear of what seemed like an endless
Cadillac.

"Owen?" Mary touched his arm and he swung the
wheel and brought his head back in to gaze at her
inquiringly. "I'd better let Jenny know that I'm
going, she's at the pool expecting me for a swim."

"But we won't even be fifteen minutes," said St.
Ives. "We'll buy anything at all that has made in
Mexico on it."

It was so at odds with him that Mary laughed a
little in spite of her growing sense of guilt. "No, I
must. She'll go all the way up to the room, dripping
and freezing, and find herself locked out."

She had the door firmly open by this time. St. Ives
glanced at his watch. "The place I had in mind will
be closing in a few minutes—"

Perhaps because of opposition, however slight,
Mary's compunction was turning into actual worry—
why, when Jenny could give lessons to a fish? Because
of that startling episode at the market? She got out
of the car, aware of a disappointment that mirrored
his, and said before she closed the door, "I'm really
sorry, but most of the shops here have quite pretty
lacy shawls. I think you're safer with that than a poncho."

"Thanks anyway," said St. Ives a trifle moodily, and
drove away.

To run to the pool would be ridiculous, now that
she hadn't left the motel after all and was on her way
to it. Mary walked rapidly along the arched passageway, emerged, found herself standing involuntarily
still and staring.

The late afternoon was warm and windless, as

100

though the weather were holding its breath for something, and there were a number of bathing-suited people on the scene but not in the water, including the two children who usually splashed so tirelessly at the shallow end. There was also a waiter, unmoving, with a tray of drinks poised at shoulder level. Daniel Brennan sat alone at a table, his chair swivelled around.

It took Mary moments to realize that in the same way in which a pair of expert dancers could clear a floor by silent and unanimous consent, Jenny had claimed the pool for herself by a virtuoso display from the diving board.

She was climbing up the ladder now, tugging briefly at her cap. Apparently oblivious of her intently watching audience, she paced along the board, positioned herself at its end with her back to the water, took a visibly deep breath, sprang high, and twisted twice before she entered the pool with almost no splash. She had evidently been doing variations of this for some time, because the tableau began to break, the erstwhile or would-be swimmers moving away, the waiter finally proceeding with his tray.

Daniel Brennan rose and came toward Mary. "That is a diver," he remarked. There was something neutral in his tone. "My friend has Mexican stomach, to put it at its politest, and we've been working in his room between groans."

Without actually taking Mary's arm he had maneuvered her to his table and pulled out a chair so naturally that she sat down without thinking. "This is my spectator sport break. I'm not—" he was barefoot, in dark blue trunks and polo shirt "—supposed to be swimming here legitimately but I did go in. What can I get you to drink?"

Owen St. Ives had had a Bacardi on the rocks waiting for her—informed by Jenny, Mary reminded herself. She asked for a gin and tonic, and Brennan picked up his own empty glass. "Quicker," he said, and started off in the direction of the bar.

Jenny was on the diving board again, out of breath but purposeful. She saw Mary, waved, ran three steps and soared off in a front flip. When she emerged again and executed a dive so complicated that it was possible to see individual muscles tense and relax and tense again as she stood in position, Mary felt a deep stir of uneasiness. Jenny had strong feelings about people who monopolized pools, which was exactly what she was doing, and in spite of her expertise in the water she wasn't an exhibitionist. Moreover, this was not an exhibition in any accepted sense; it was something grim and driving and joyless. She was, thought Mary, like someone who has received a severe shock and starts scrubbing the house with furious, vacant energy.

Daniel Brennan came back with their drinks. It must have occurred to him that Mary might wonder why two men with business to transact occupied different motels, because he said as he set the glasses down, "I stayed here once shortly after they opened. I got the impression that they were paying me, and I'd better look sharp."

He studied Mary's expression and followed her gaze to the ladder which the claret-suited figure, lean as a whip if a whip could have bones, was climbing again. He said, still with that detached air, "She

—Jenny, did you say?—has been at this for at least half an hour."

Easily that, while Mary had found no one home at the Taylors', learned from Mrs. Ulibarri that there had been no inquiring strangers of any variety, almost gone off with Owen St. Ives on his present-buying errand. All in all, it had been a frustrating period of time. And what to do now about a situation which was beginning to rasp at her nerves? Jenny was far too old to approach as one would a child with whom wild mirth and activity meant certain tears to come—not that there was any mirth in what she was doing, but there was the same sense of an attitude slipped out of control.

Something to do with that glimpse in the market, or even with—

Brennan's glass went down with a crash. He said unbelievingly, "She hasn't—"

His chair fell over backwards as he raced the few yards to the pool and shot over the edge, not in one of Jenny's neat entries but with an echoing, cracking splash. At any other time Mary would have winced for someone hitting the water with that impact. Now she ran after him, chest hurting and thudding as if someone were beating on it from the outside, caught up in a kind of terror entirely new to her. ("Aunt Henrietta, I don't know how to tell you this . . .")

There was an underwater tangle of arms and legs, of dark blue and claret, and then Jenny's white-capped head broke the surface and her neck was encircled in the crook of Brennan's arm. Her face was contorted with coughing as he back-pedalled with her to standing depth. Sealed off from any real

103

interest of Mary's was the fact that he looked grim and furious.

She got down on the concrete, partly because her legs felt unreliable, surprised at the effort required not to cry because with her strange mixture of blitheness and sardonicism Jenny had so nearly—"Oh, Jenny. Are you all right?"

Jenny nodded, unable to speak through her convulsive coughing. There was a red graze on her forehead just under the edge of her cap, startling against her total pallor. In spite of her shaken appearance, she gave the impression of having been jarred back to normal. Brennan looked down at her and said, "Okay now?" and, his grip not particularly gentle, helped her up the steps.

For Mary, the world still hummed and spun. "Come and sit down for a minute, Jenny. You must be—"

"I'm fine," said Jenny, pulling off her cap and trying for an approximation of her melting smile. She couldn't manage it. "Stupid, but fine." For the first time, she took in the fact of Mary's dress. "I thought you were coming for a swim."

If she had, might this dangerous mood have been at least diluted? "I was, but I got sidetracked," said Mary, because she could hardly explain her long and fruitless interval on the telephone. Something seemed to be badly missing from this scene, and she turned to Daniel Brennan, who had stripped off his polo shirt and seemed illogically to be trying to dry his hands on it. "I'm so glad you were here and watching. We can't thank you enough."

"You could have dinner with me tonight," suggested Brennan surprisingly. He had rearranged his face into amiability. "That is if Jenny's up to it."

"Oh, I'll be up to it," said Jenny, airy, and sauntered away. The few observers were drifting off too, glancing over their shoulders. One of the two children said to the other with fascination and overtones of regret, "She almost drownded."

Brennan heard. "She probably would have made it by herself," he said, and seemed to feel a trace of reaction. "If I were a drinking man . . . for someone so much at home in the water, Jenny put up quite a fight. Fortunately, I am a drinking man. Seven-thirty, or should I call you, just in case?"

"Better call," said Mary, although it was Jenny who had done the accepting, "and thank you again."

She collected Jenny's terry robe and straw bag, and made a firm, unscrupulous resolution to see for herself the message from Astrid as soon as she was out of sight. Now that she thought about it, it would be only natural to show a thank-you note for a ride to the person who owned the car and had done the driving, and something had triggered that wildness in Jenny.

The bag was already unzipped—and here was Jenny, coming back along the passageway. "Oh, you got my things. Thanks." She seemed to be braced for a lecture of some sort, because she said rapidly as they mounted the stairs, "I dove too deep—Acton, Girl Show-off—and I knew there was nobody else in the pool and I got sort of in a panic when I saw Mr. Brennan coming at me. I'm sorry, Mary, I won't do it again."

Something told Mary that Jenny did not often apologize, so she only said mildly, "I'd take it very

105

kindly." Now that it was all over, she felt extraordinarily trembly; such events, she thought, wobbling the key into its hole, could be harder on the spectator than the participant. In their room, she examined the scrape on her cousin's forehead. "Are you sure you're all right? Not dizzy or anything?"

"No, and I'm not going to throw up, either. Honestly, stop worrying about me. The Actons are famous for their thick skulls," said Jenny with a bitterness that her light tone didn't conceal, and went into the bathroom to change. It was clear that she wanted the incident closed, and equally clear that any question as to what had led to her singular behavior would be met by an air of baffled innocence.

She took the straw handbag with her instead of dumping it on the floor beside her chair as she usually did. The next sound you hear, Mary said to herself, will be that of notepaper being torn into tiny, flushable pieces. She was wrong; the sound she heard, and which shot her upright, was entirely different.

10

It was like a private and fleeting roll of thunder, and it came from someone falling heavily against the other side of the locked communicating door directly behind the chair in which Mary was sitting.

She was instantly out of the chair, holding up a silencing hand as the bathroom door opened and Jenny's startled face emerged. Concentrating, she could hear a man's voice, controlled but urgent. "Come away from there."

Mumble, also male.

"Come away!"

After a few seconds there was the quiet but distinct closing of a door, not on the corridor. Mary realized for the first time why there was so relatively little coming and going on the stairs: those invisible occupants had taken the adjoining room as well, although until now there hadn't been so much as a whisper from it. There was a bumper sticker which read

107

"Help! The paranoids are after me," but this seemed to be a case of the real thing.

Jenny was still staring, her unconcern pierced at last. "All this place needs is little bunches of garlic over the doors and windows to keep vampires out."

"I think you're right," said Mary with feeling. She tried to be entertained at the notion of Dracula in sombrero and serape, but remembered instead the nonchalance with which the employees here attempted to use passkeys. She looked at the decorative little chain on the door: a determined child could get past it. For purposes of security, they might as well be living in a paper bag.

Had someone, moments ago, thought to hurl himself into this room? Would he try from the corridor? "It will be a horrible nuisance to pack everything up," said Mary, "but I'm going to see if they can put us elsewhere."

The door-chains were undoubtedly standard throughout the motel, but at least she and Jenny would be removed from the now unnerving presence which was so much closer than she had thought. She started for the telephone, and Jenny said tentatively, "Or we could go back tonight."

Mary shook her head firmly at that. She found night driving taxing even with a companion to ward off drowsiness, and the prospect of long hours of it, with stretches of divided highway turning suddenly into two-way traffic and Jenny almost certainly fast asleep, was unthinkable. In any case, the problem that had brought them down here wasn't resolved. She lifted the receiver, and put her request.

Expectably, the clerk did not ask what was wrong

108

with the present room, so that it might be corrected, nor did he inquire about the state of the lamp. He simply assured Mary that there was no other accommodation in the motel, and sounded amazed that she could think there might be. He was not her familiar adversary, for whom she was developing a certain admiration, or he would have added a bland, "Lo siento."

Because even this token regret was lacking, and to test his reaction, Mary said that surely the room next to theirs was unoccupied?

There wasn't so much as a flicker of hesitation, let alone a pause to consult a chart, although the Casa de Flores must have contained at least fifty rooms. Two-thirty-eight, said the clerk at once, formed part of a suite and was most certainly occupied.

Mary replaced the receiver and sat down on her bed with the Juarez directory. As with any half-formed decision, her resolution had hardened in the face of an obstacle, and her distaste for this room, and in fact for this whole place, had grown proportionately—or, she supposed, disproportionately. But there it was: she hadn't liked the Casa de Flores from the moment she set foot in it, and this new circumstance was a violent underscoring.

Had the same man caused that half-cry in the night? And from whom? It needn't have been during the small hours. Fatigue distorted the time sense, so that bar service might still have been available and a waiter have encountered—what?

Someone all bandages, like the Invisible Man? In the throes of drug withdrawal the hard way? With two heads? Mary put her nerves severely back into place and found the number of one of the American chain motels. The telephone rang as she stretched out her hand to it.

She expected the clerk, prepared to move them after some upper-echelon consultation because this was clearly a touchy area in the motel. Instead, Owen St. Ives said, "Mary?" It was the first time he had used her name. "Someone told me there was an incident at the pool, and from the description it can only have been Jenny. Is she all right?"

Mary felt an odd but recognizable sensation, twin to the one she had experienced in the early days when Spence, after they had quarrelled on their way to a party, had attached himself to a girl with waist-length copper hair until he learned that she not only owned but fully intended later on to play the harp standing ominously in a corner. She said, mentally arming herself against any more surprises in this vein, "Yes, luckily," and then, as Jenny emerged from the bathroom, "Hold on a second, here she is."

Jenny's eyebrows went up in surprise. "Owen St. Ives," murmured Mary, and handed over the receiver which, she realized belatedly, had come alive again with his voice in the tiny interval of transition. Ostentatiously busy and unlistening, she measured herself a drink to take the place of the one untasted beside the pool.

She had already learned not to think seriously about ice here. She added water to her Bacardi, and there at her feet was Jenny's straw bag, abandoned in her curiosity at the ringing of the hitherto silent room telephone. It was unzipped as before—a technicality—and approximately thirty seconds ago Mary

110

would have bent for it instantly. Now, because of some brand-new and complicated reaction, she had to force herself to remember those moments of terror while she stared at the water, and the very real fact that with a little more impetus in that downward plunge Jenny might have broken her neck.

But the note that had to be the cause of it all, purportedly from Astrid, wasn't there, at least in a fast search. Put that beside Jenny's proposal that they leave Juarez tonight and you got—what?

"Mary?" Jenny had the mouthpiece of the receiver against her palm, and her eyes looked beseeching. "He wants to know if we'll have dinner with him."

"We're already committed," said Mary, not pointing out that it was Jenny who had done the committing, "and I do think that under the circumstances—"

"Mr. Brennan doesn't want *me,*" said Jenny, explaining it kindly. "He was only being polite."

It was true that his invitation to Jenny had lacked enthusiasm; evidently he hadn't appreciated that underwater tussle. "Whichever you want, then, it's up to you," said Mary.

She half-regretted the words as soon as they were out, even though it would scarcely be possible to forbid Jenny to do anything. Couldn't it be considered a trifle odd that the day after their arrival here they were dining separately with people who were in effect strangers? Or was that simply a carry-over, a false echo of the feeling of imminence that had driven her out of St. Ives's car? Yes, because it was only the briefly shared responsibility at the pool which had prompted Daniel Brennan's invitation.

The receiver went down with a little click, cutting

off what had been for Mary an undeciphered pattern of words. "He's going to meet me downstairs at seven-fifteen," said Jenny. "You don't really mind, do you?"

"Not at all, but," said Mary, entirely reasonable, "I think you ought to make it a fairly early evening after that bang on the head."

Jenny gave her a glance which might have contained amusement, moved to the mirror, stared, bent closer. Any amusement departed. "Good God, what am I going to do about this? It looks like the mark of Cain."

The graze on her forehead had indeed darkened and acquired a kind of tight burnish. Mary said, "Well, makeup . . ."

"An inch of it?"

There was a gift shop in the lobby which might conceivably harbor something other than souvenirs at exorbitant prices. Mary offered to try to locate a Band-aid, as she was going down for a newspaper anyway, and Jenny muttered, "Oh, I'd look great in a Band-aid, with maybe some grass-stains and a skinned elbow to go with it."

Mary left her still peering into the mirror. She had no intention of buying a newspaper, but in view of the tacit truce achieved after that scene in the market it did not seem wise to mention the actual and elementary mission which had occurred to her.

The sky to the south was eggplant-colored and a precursory little wind had sprung up. It was going to rain again, and soon. At this hour the forecourt was more than crowded with cars; two foreign compacts were sealed in by the careless length of a Lincoln

112

with Texas plates. Mary counted seven blue ones, none of them resembling the one which had stayed so long in her rear-view mirror.

The auxiliary area where she had had to park that afternoon contained three blue cars, all unfamiliar. It didn't prove anything. If the vehicle in question did have some connection with Jenny, if in a tit-for-tat gesture Brian Beardsley had hired someone to trail her, it might be parked somewhere on a side street. Still, if Mary had listened to this tale from someone else, she would have said incredulously, "You mean she suspected this car and she didn't even look to see if it was right there at the motel? She can't be very bright."

The air darkened subtly, and a discarded paper cup and a corkscrewed cigarette package spun erratically across the asphalt in what might almost have been the wind of Brian Beardsley's passing. Because Mary, standing there in the parking area, was suddenly and paradoxically sure to her bones that he was here in Juarez and that Jenny had seen him that afternoon.

She told herself that she ought to feel reassured. The enemy had been encountered, certainly without prearrangement, and right now, upstairs, Jenny was solely absorbed in how to disguise the injury brought about by her own frightening recklessness. She was skilled at evasion, but there could be no doubt about her eagerness to dine with Owen St. Ives. Before the arising of that circumstance, she had seemed anxious to leave Juarez; now, she might be hoping that Beardsley would see them together.

On the other hand, he hadn't come all this way for

nothing. The very lack of any overt move could be interpreted as purposeful—spiders did not build noisy webs—and Mary's dislike of the Casa de Flores, and even this deserted area in which she stood, changed to something much sharper.

She went back the way she had come, running a little now and then; to get out of the wind, she assured herself. Jenny, opening to her knock, said self-consciously, "No paper? Mr. Brennan phoned a minute ago, he's going to call back."

"Oh." Mary hoped she had not stared, as at an apparition. "You've, er, cut your hair, I see. It looks nice."

It wasn't quite the proper description. Using Mary's manicure scissors, Jenny had sawed her hair into bangs to cover the offending graze. The slightly uneven black fringe, too short, robbed her long narrow face of its individuality, like the before-and-after cosmetic ads which undertook to bring all features within the limits of an arbitrary norm. Mary was reminded of a tall spindly comedienne doing a little-girl impression; only a huge bow and Mary Janes were missing.

"I look horrible, I know," said Jenny, desperately nonchalant, and Mary, recognizing that this was not the moment to observe that at least she had gotten rid of a lot of split ends, assured her that on the contrary the effect was quite—she hunted for a word which might beguile—dashing.

Under other circumstances she would have taken the inadequate scissors in hand and softened the T-square angles at her cousin's temples. Now, she sat down on her bed with the directory and announced her intention of finding another motel for the night: "The longer I stay in this place, the less I like it, and I've just remembered a place we might be able to get into."

Jenny gazed in consternation. "But what about dinner?"

"It's still early." Mary was ruffling through the pages to the J's. "We can dress and pack and I'll take the bags over while you wait downstairs."

Here it was: Jaime's Hotel, almost in town and on a main street, where she had stayed on two or three occasions and to which in case of necessity she had a mysterious entree, as yet untried, passed on by a friend. Jaime's had none of the pretension of the Casa de Flores. Its paint was in need of repair, its beds made protesting sounds, its upholstered-appearing chairs were apt to send an unwary sitter ricocheting. But the two-storied annex where Mary had always stayed was built around a flagstoned center court-yard where the swimming pool was willow-hung and flower-fringed, and the atmosphere was friendly and the food good. Mary sometimes suspected that its raucous neon sign and the faintly raffish pink light emanating from it at night were deceptions: Jaime's did not need to woo tourists for its survival.

Two minutes later, having been informed politely that there were no vacancies, she was testing her ploy. "I see. Would it be possible—" she made it sound unrelated, an afterthought, so as not to spoil this game for future comers "—to speak to Raoul?"

Surprisingly, for all its amateur-detective air, it worked. A courteous voice which was Raoul's came on after a short wait, and after Mary had identified herself as a friend of the Julian Bells in Santa Fe there was a further little pause and then, "A double room with bath . . . Yes. About seven-thirty?"

Jenny, poised with a pink dress over her arm to await the outcome of the call, made a pleased zero in the air with thumb and forefinger and withdrew. Mary said a warm thank you to the unknown Raoul and hung up, resolving to take back a bottle of gin for the martini-drinking Bells. Which reminded her of her own barely touched drink; she moved across the room to it, and was suddenly in the exact spot where she had stood that morning after washing the spilled coffee out of her clothes. She had been very briefly bothered then, as if she were neglecting something which ought to be done, and now she knew what it was.

Her suitcase, closed but not locked because she had long ago lost the key. She had defended the chambermaid to Jenny, but her mind had obviously made a note of its own because in a gesture alien to her—it had never crossed her mind before to distrust a maid—she carried the suitcase to the bed (Had there been an edge of fabric protruding from it that morning? There wasn't now), opened it, inspected the contents.

She was found of her gold heishi earrings and a sand-cast silver pair, but they were hardly goals for theft and they were there, nestled in the side zippered compartment. Nor did it look—Mary found herself remembering the woman's silent, sloping glide—as though the suitcase had been prowled through.

Jenny issued forth in her pink dress, bangs firmly

116

damped down, mildly inquisitive at the sight of Mary contemplating her own belongings as though they were the work of an old master. Mary said, "It's just occurred to me that people are very fast with their passkeys here and you're travelling around with your grandmother's pearls. Do you keep your suitcase locked?"

Jenny shook her head; like Mary, probably like a great many other people, she had lost the key. "But I'm not a hundred per cent crazy." She drew out an apparently unopened package of pantyhose, slipped her fingers inside and extracted the single strand of quietly shimmering pearls, which she fastened at once about her throat. "Foiled again," she said fondly.

So Mary, forgetting the fact that there were two actions possible with suitcases, dismissed the matter from her mind. She dressed, found a childish satisfaction in phoning downstairs to have her bill prepared, told Daniel Brennan when he called that they were moving to Jaime's Hotel and that she would meet him there at seven-thirty.

"*Jaime's?*" The telephone wire conveyed as much astonishment as a facial expression. "That's where I'm phoning from, as a matter of fact . . . No Jenny?"

How easily and frequently they used her name. It did not enter Mary's head that, for purposes of striking up an acquaintance, her cousin was as made-to-order as an exotic dog on a leash. To avoid any misapprehension, she said that Jenny had turned out to have dinner plans of her own, an obvious lie in view of that offhand acceptance at the pool, and realized as she was speaking that Brennan hadn't sounded disappointed but only formally polite.

He suggested a restaurant new to Mary—"If you have a raincoat, that is. Otherwise . . ."

Mary, who had been conscious for some time of the ticking, prickling sounds against the window, replied that she did. So, fortunately for the plan she had devised on her way back from the parking area, did Jenny. In it, in spite of her storklike legs, she was not nearly as noticeable.

"Out to kill," remarked Jenny suddenly. She had been inspecting her own blue eyeliner the moment before; now, in the mirror, she was studying Mary in thin sauterne-wool only slightly paler than her hair, the skirt swaying as she moved, only the earrings with their vertical hyphens of gold for accent.

"No, just to stun," said Mary ironically. "I'll be right back, I'm going to settle up at the desk."

Her bill was in error by two dollars and eighty cents. To the clerk who corrected it with a practiced air of amazement and apology, she was at pains to explain that they were checking out because Miss Acton's accident at the pool was turning out to be a little more serious than they had thought, and it seemed wise to get her back to her own doctor at once.

She had expected this to sink in, and it did. The clerk was instantly on guard, pointing out with much raising of shoulders and eyebrows that a posted sign advised divers that they were at their own risk. He would remember them and their destination homeward quite well, now, in case a man inquired for Jennifer Acton. Mary paid her bill, and turned to find herself gazing at Owen St. Ives.

118

How much of that had he heard? He was certainly looking attentive, as well he might, expecting to take the invalid out to dinner momentarily. "Jenny will be down in a minute," said Mary, moving out of earshot of the desk. "Did you—" she smiled at him briskly, the gift counsellor who had been called away to other duties "—get your shopping done?"

St. Ives nodded. "I took your advice about a shawl." His dark blue gaze stayed on Mary's. "I'm sorry you can't join us, but I understand there's a friend."

He used the term in its comprehensive context rather than that of a single engagement. (Jenny's work? "Your Mr. Brennan?") Mary didn't explain, partly because the lobby was beginning to be criss-crossed by people meeting other people for drinks or dinner, and the bellboy whom the clerk had summoned had spread his feet and clasped his hands behind his back with the air of a man whose patience was wearing dangerously thin. "I'm sorry too. Good night," she said, and glanced back involuntarily as she reached the glass doors. Absurdly, she had expected him to be gazing after her. Instead, he was talking to the desk clerk.

There was nothing coy about Jenny. Thoroughly dressed and ready to depart, she greeted Mary in mid-corridor with the frantic announcement that she was going to be late; from her tone, Owen St. Ives might have been prepared to leave on the dot without her, as implacably as a train or a bus. Mary assured her that he was waiting, said, "Jaime's Hotel, remember, it's on Panama Street," and watched her flash around the turn for the stairs.

She had already made her automatic inspection of bathroom, closet, bureau drawers, and managed to squeeze the books into their luggage. Five minutes later she was out in the chilly, rainy parking lot, the suitcases in the trunk of the car, the bellboy tipped, her keys in her hand.

She retained a gratifying memory of her own insouciant wave at the watchful eye that had peered out from that other room at the sound of all those footsteps; the door had shut so sharply that it was a wonder he hadn't caught his nose. She also realized, as she closed herself into the car and inserted the ignition key, that in spite of her last-minute check for belongings she had left her faithful Juarez-travelling, fruit-peeling knife behind her on the desk.

Buy a new one tomorrow; she certainly wasn't going all the way back up to her room even if there had been time. In fact, after several dull metallic grinds in which the engine didn't turn over, she wasn't going anywhere, at least in this car. For the second time in her three-year ownership of it, the first having been on a morning when the temperature was six below zero, it had failed her.

She got out into the dark.

The other and unsuspected knife in her life, a switch-blade not used for slicing limes but for driving deep between rib-bones, had on Gil Candelaria's hunch been discovered in a now-dried abode brick in a form in the suspect's back yard. Candelaria and a deputy had had to break a number of innocent bricks before they found it. Leroy Romero's mother had begun to cry when the adobe broke away from the metal; his father had straightened his shoulders briefly before he let them droop again. In both reactions, there was a kind of terrible relief.

Even to the naked eye, the knife hadn't been washed thoroughly, but then Leroy Romero was young, arrogant, and, in charge of loading and delivering the bricks, confident of his ability to extract the one that mattered. They weren't made here on a large scale; it was a family enterprise, and the buyers were neighbors engaged in minor construction like walls or repairs to existing walls. Candelaria bore his prize away, reflecting that the elder Romeros, not cowed by poverty or incessant hard work but by their son, had deserved better.

Although it would take time for the analysis to come through from the police laboratory, Candelaria felt sure enough to let the dead woman's husband know that what they had every reason to believe was the murder weapon had been found. He fished through his papers on the case, located the number, dialled.

. . . No answer.

But of course he would be at the funeral home.

11

" . . . so I had to take a taxi," finished Mary a little breathlessly to Daniel Brennan in the lobby of Jaime's Hotel.

It was comfortably unchanged from her last visit, and a far cry from its counterpart at the Casa de Flores. There were what appeared to be the same rubber plants in the windows facing the street, and a small pink-lighted fountain in an alcove beside the stairs still let out a ratchety complaint under its splashing. The far end was in semidarkness out of deference to a televised baseball game being watched by a few dim, absorbed shapes. The bellboy was also familiar, with his long mobile face which might have belonged to a mime; in fact, Mary had never seen another bellboy here, although others must exist.

Brennan was considering the rain-ruffled hair and color-stung cheeks she had already seen reflected in the mirror behind the desk. "Would you rather have dinner here, in view of the weather? I made reservations at the other place, but they're easily cancelled."

"No, not at all, if you don't mind driving in the rain." Mary felt actually exhilarated by it and the accompanying drop in temperature; it was hard to believe that she had been prepared to swim that afternoon. "I'll be down in just a few minutes."

Once again, she was not going to be housed in the hotel proper. The bellboy, keeping solicitously under the roof overhang as long as possible, conducted her across a stretch of puddled flagstones, past the pool, and up a flight of wooden stairs with a railing no shakier than she remembered it. The room, a corner one, looked more like space at a summer camp than a hotel accommodation. In spite of tautly drawn coverlets the twin beds had a faintly undulant appearance, the two no-colored chairs managed not to match, desk and chest of drawers were baldly just those. There was only a shower, but in that respect Mary had lost nothing. This place seemed honest and safe after the false sumptuousness of the Casa de Flores, and she liked every inch of it.

She said curiously as the bellboy placed the heavier of the two suitcases on the luggage rack, "Thank you, this is very nice. I've been here before, but could you tell me who Raoul is?"

He gave her a shy and charming smile and a little bow. "I am Raoul. How are Mr. and Mrs. Bell?"

Mary, released from embarrassment by his tact, said that they were fine and Julian Bell had just had a new book published. "Ah," said Raoul admiringly while between them the tip was managed with great delicacy. "If you should need anything, madame . . ."

He indicated the telephone and withdrew. A relative of the management? Or someone on the staff so long that he had a room at his own discretion? It was probably, thought Mary, going to the mirror for brief repairs to her hair and face, one of those mysteries better left unexplored. But she must ask him at the first opportunity the best garage to call about her car.

She had been lucky, finding a taxi almost at once although the rain was by then coming down in earnest. The suitcases were manageable, even with the books inside. A couple festive in dress but not in mood were being decanted as she reached the motel front; the woman had snarled as Mary climbed in, "I suppose your precious Mavis Jean will be here," and the man had replied tersely, "Shut up, you hear?" (Shouldn't that have been "You-all shut up?")

. . . In the courtyard, pool and willows received the rain in rustly near-silence; the flagstones were loud with it. People here parked like mad sardines because of the inadequate space, and as Mary reached the bottom of the wooden stairs one driver was in the process of extricating himself from what seemed an impossible corner. It proved to be Brennan. As she passed in front of his headlights Mary held up her room key, ran inside, left it at the desk with the explanation that Miss Acton might be requiring it first, and, moments later, was in the car which had cruised successfully up to the rear entrance.

"That was a fast few minutes," observed Brennan, mildly congratulatory. He steered through the narrow gate and made a surprising left turn. "About your car—were you thinking of going back tomorrow?"

Was she? No, thought Mary instantly, realizing that this decision had already been made in her subconscious mind. After all this trouble, and all this nervousness, she had to give Brian Beardsley time to learn at the Casa de Flores that Jenny was on her way or had already returned to Santa Fe, try to find her at the house there, realize that he was being eluded and—surely?—give up. He might be furious at the Actons, but he couldn't very well devote an indefinite period of time to the arranging of some personal revenge; for all he knew, Mary had any number of sheltering, cooperating friends.

She started to say, "It depends—" but she had hesitated too long. Daniel Brennan said a little stiffly, "Because I'd be glad to have a look in the morning. It might be something simple."

"It didn't sound like that, but thank you very much, I'd appreciate it."

Was there an inoffensive way to inquire if he knew where he was going? The lights of the Avenue of the Sixteenth of September, named after Mexican Independence Day, with its lively concentration of shops and restaurants and nightclubs, were steadily receding as the car threaded its way through narrow back streets. Mary liked driving here by day—the national tendency to decorate even the most utilitarian structure was a constant pleasure—but at night, in the rain, there was something secretive and even a little hostile about the shrouded windows behind iron grillwork, an occasional door whisked open and swiftly shut on a pulse of music, black alley-mouths which could lead anywhere.

She took a quick side glance at Brennan's profile, and at once, as if he had been anticipating her as he had at the pool or because the silence in the car seemed to be assuming an actual shape, he turned his head. "Sorry, I'm not getting us there very fast, am I? Some idiot gave me directions for what he said was a short cut, but he must have had Chihuahua in mind."

"I think—" began Mary circumspectly, and stopped, because Brennan had brought the car to an idling halt on the empty one-way street. He fished in a pocket, brought out not the scribbled map she expected but cigarettes, seemed not to know what to do with them, stuffed them away again. These maneuvers had brought him around in the seat so that he half-faced her. He is not the kind of man to make random passes, thought Mary, but her shoulders had stiffened involuntarily against the seat.

"I might as well tell you," said Brennan, casual and astonishing, "that Jenny is quite right. About not trusting me, I mean."

Jenny, tall and sprawly, childish and sardonic by turns—this was a flashback from the pool—coming along like an invisible third. Couldn't she be content with Owen St. Ives? After this initial reaction, as instinctive as ducking from a flung missile but still shocking to her, Mary realized that Jenny did not in fact appear to care much for Daniel Brennan—but wasn't that a compound of pique, at having been paid very little attention to upon introduction, and chagrin at the necessity for the pool rescue? He was after all an attractive man, and at the moment all

Jenny's pores were open.

Why had he picked this unlikely time and place for his challenge, as awkward to answer as the one about wife-beating? The motor idled expectantly. Voice deliberately light, Mary said, "There must have been a more reassuring way to put that," and then Brennan's face seemed to spring at her as the windshield was caught in an explosion of light.

There was a long shriek of tires from the car coming at them the wrong way, invisible behind its flaring, dazzling beams; a jolt as Brennan rammed his car into gear and wrenched it to the right and up over the curb; a thin tearing sound of metal against metal, a heavy shudder and then, almost daintily, a tinkle of falling glass. And, for just a second, heart-adjusting, nerve-reacting silence.

Brennan was wordlessly out of the car, slamming the door behind him with force. Mary, chest still hammering with left-over alarm, could understand his wrath: if he hadn't stopped the car, if they had been approaching the corner, a head-on collision would have been inevitable. She twisted in her seat to peer through the rain-pebbled rear window, and saw Brennan walking toward a man and woman standing defensively against the glare from their remaining headlight. A dialogue commenced, Brennan with his head down and his hands pushed into his pockets as though commanding himself to be quiet.

The woman detached herself and came to bend and look in at Mary, who rolled the window down. Short gray curls and ruddy face under a plastic rain hat: this was one of the group at the Casa de Flores.

127

The recognition was mutual. "You're at the motel, aren't you," asked the woman, "with that very sk—, I mean that very slender girl? My husband is just explaining that the one-way sign up there is bent and we didn't see it until too late. I hope you didn't get too shook up?"

She was jaunty with nerves. Mary said no, politely; what about her?

"Oh, this has been a trip, let me tell you," said the woman elliptically. She bent closer. "Do you get the feeling that we're being watched by maybe seven hundred people?"

It was true, thought Mary. Although the only witnesses bodily on the scene were a trio of small boys who had appeared with magical swiftness, the night felt alive with eyes, possibly scornful ones. Anglos coming over the border to buy liquor inexpensively (although Texas exacted its bite, even from non-Texans), feeling free to misbehave as they wouldn't at home . . . She felt more than ever like an intruder.

All at once, as abruptly as it had arisen, the incident was over. The rain-hatted woman vanished in response to an indistinct hail, car doors slammed, Brennan got in beside Mary and switched on the ignition. "I'm sorry," he said, glancing at her. "So much for short cuts in strange places. I guarantee that we'll have a drink in hand, one way or another, within the next ten minutes."

His tone was free of temper, his hands on the wheel were not. In view of a strange and hollow thumping from the rear at every unevenness in the street, and there were many, Mary thought it diplomatic not to inquire about the extent of the car's

128

damage. Brennan volunteered it after a block or two, his taut grip relaxing. "We're not really falling apart, the bumper got ripped loose at one end. What's the matter?" he asked sharply as Mary leaned forward and stared past him at a brightly lighted corner.

"Nothing, I just saw someone from the motel," said Mary inadequately. She craned back as Brennan completed his turn onto the main street, but the doors of the nightclub had already closed upon Astrid and the extraordinary man with her.

Over a drink, secured almost within the limits of the guarantee, Mary told Brennan about Astrid, omitting out of loyalty her own conviction that the girl's note had a direct connection with Jenny's self-destructive urge on the diving board. "The man she was with certainly isn't her uncle," she ended. "He—"

Brennan waited, absorbed, attentive, and Mary realized that she had only started on this at all to dilute the disturbing intensity with which he had studied her across a room instead of across a table the evening before. It came home to her too that to describe Astrid's companion as dark-blond and fairly tall would be meaningless, like describing a chair as having four legs.

It was true that she had had only one fast glimpse of that surprising face, but there were faces—or the personalities stamped on them as indivisibly as the light in which they were viewed—for which one glimpse was enough. Further observation could not enhance but only dull the initial impact.

"They are," said Mary considering it carefully, "a matched pair."

Brennan nodded comprehendingly. He remembered Astrid from the motel dining room, and now he suggested, "She spotted this dazzling fellow, a case of like meeting like, and persuaded her relatives to stay on after all. She looks like a girl who gets her own way without even trying."

It was an accurate observation, and a fresh drink was set before them and Brennan was recommending the roast beef. In a small clear interlude a voice at the next table said, " . . . six *years,* and that was for a couple of joints! Have you any idea what these prisons are like?"

The restaurant was expensive, and Mary thought it was time to contribute something to the evening. She asked Daniel Brennan if he came to Juarez often, and he said no, only once or twice a year, in connection with the small prestigious shop in Santa Fe of which he was the business half. Mary, who knew the shop, was somehow surprised. It was the kind of deliberately daunting place that displayed only a very few items at a time—a white basket-work pottery wedding bowl from Acoma Pueblo, or micaceous pottery with the sheen of copper from Picuris, or beaten silver or intricately wrought gold from Mexico. All without price tags, so that to inquire seemed a statement of inability to pay.

Brennan smiled over his glass. "I agree," he said to what must have been Mary's weighing expression, "but it's very successful. And no worse, you must admit, than those women's shops where you sit down and an ex-countess goes off and comes back with three dresses."

"Oh, you know about those."

"Yes." It was said with finality. "And what about you? If you know about Jaime's you must be a fairly old hand . . ."

Was it the superlative roast beef, the icy Carta Blanca ordered with it, the shared near-accident on the way here? Or, more realistically, the brandy? For whatever reason, there came a point when Mary heard herself saying suddenly, "You mentioned something, before, about Jenny being right not to trust you. I can't help wondering how the rest of that goes."

The moment it was said, she wished it back. The man at the next table was going on angrily, " . . . had to pay for his own crummy *bed,* for God's sake, and not an official finger lifted to help. You think he's going to forget that?"

Brennan caught Mary's gaze with his own. "Somehow I liked this better in the car . . . I was never introduced to you. I'd never even seen you before, although I can't imagine why. I was in the lobby when you arrived with Jenny, and I wanted very much to meet you. You don't look approachable by strange men, so I asked the desk clerk, who got your name wrong, and when you weren't in the dining room I thought I'd take a chance on Armand's, because it's the nearest restaurant, and there you were."

He gave a self-critical shrug. "Adolescent, at best. At worst, travelling-salesman. 'Haven't we met before?' I don't, I assure you, make a practice of it."

Mary, at something of a loss because he was now openly cataloguing her features as if to remind himself of what had attracted him, or maybe to wonder

131

what had made him bother at all, found her face growing hot for the second time that day. Worse, in self-conscious situations like this, she was unable to return a gaze naturally; people's eyes separated themselves suddenly into the right and the left, and it was a decision as to which eye to address.

Their brandy was long finished, and she took refuge in bending for her bag, dropping her cigarettes and lighter into it, saying, "Well, thank you very much—" ambiguous slide into the next phrase "—for a marvelous dinner."

Brennan didn't demur at these unmistakable gestures toward departure. He caught their waiter's attention and made a scribbling motion in the air, and the waiter came with a promptitude reminiscent of lunch at the Casa de Flores, when Astrid had only to lift her eyes to be supplied almost at once with a daiquiri.

And that was all, Mary realized with a clarity that had escaped her at the time. Astrid had indicated that she and some companions would be ordering lunch—but long before there would have been any chance of its arriving she had been in the lobby, talking to Jenny in front of the postcard display. She must simply have put down money for the cocktail.

And two hours after that she had written a note to Jenny. Or someone had.

. . . The man with Astrid, tonight. A Pied Piper's face, thought Mary, totally unaware of Daniel Brennan's curious glance on her own. Indescribable, really, although you could apply certain adjectives. Pointed, with circumflex eyebrows and a cleft in the chin. Dark-blond hair in a kind of helmet effect

132

which wasn't in the least womanish or, for that matter, hippie-ish. Arm negligently around Astrid, hand resting on her curvy hip.

Brian Beardsley.

Something had tugged vaguely at Mary's mind upon that meeting in the lobby, and now it presented itself with precision. There was nothing in the least babyish about Astrid, she had thought at the time—and unconsciously been balancing Jenny's vulnerability against sure accomplishment. More: if you searched the earth, it would be hard to find two more dissimilar types than tall, loose-jointed Jenny and cuddle-able little Astrid. Even without her cousin's starvation campaign, they were like a bold charcoal drawing and an oil of sun-warmed fruit and wine. What a triumph, for a man still stinging from his summary treatment at the Actons' hands, to flourish Astrid at Jenny, to demonstrate in the most convincing way possible that what had been an upheaval in her life had been an unimportant episode in his.

Which was exactly what he hadn't done. In fact, as it would be highly unlikely for two women to go unescorted to a Juarez nightclub, it was the purest chance that Mary herself had seen the two of them at all.

". . . Ready?" The check had been paid, the tray with its tip pushed to one side, from an echolike effect on the air Brennan had asked this for the second time. Mary gathered herself at once, saying, "Oh, yes, sorry," and allowing only one last stray speculation as her coat was held for her. She had wondered, when Jenny retailed the contents of the note, how Astrid had compressed her message into

133

what was undeniably a single line. She had even seen the handwriting on the envelope, blue and sweeping, and hadn't made the connection.

What had Brian Beardsley said to Jenny, using Astrid—satisfying stroke—as addresser and courier as well?

The rain had stopped, but the gutters rushed with it, and the sidewalks were deeply pooled. Twice on the way to the car Brennan gave Mary an assisting arm, his firm impersonal grip falling away at once. Normally, she would have tried to make amends on the drive back to the hotel; he had after all bought her an expensive dinner, getting his car damaged in the process, and she had rewarded him—and on the heels of that surprising explanation of his behavior— by withdrawing her attention as thoroughly as if she had left the table.

But the circumstances weren't normal, and hadn't been since she had answered the telephone in Santa Fe forty-eight hours ago. Logic spelled out a perfectly safe equation—Brian Beardsley with Astrid, Jenny with Owen St. Ives—but Mary tensed with impatience at a red light, an enforced crawl behind a bus, a stalled car creating a knot of traffic. Moreover, although he saw to it that they did not travel in utter silence, Daniel Brennan had gone into a retreat of his own. He was obviously a man to whom any real or imagined rebuff from a woman presented not a challenge but an occasion for civil goodbyes.

A van blocking the entrance to Jaime's courtyard, its luridly painted tiger-eyes glittering with raindrops, was the last straw. Brennan sounded his horn in accordance with the notice on the wall-corner, but

Mary already had a hand on the door release. "Would you mind . . .? It's getting late, and I'm anxious to see if Jenny is back."

It wasn't really late; it only felt that way to newly awakened nerves. And, thought Mary irrelevantly, they hadn't addressed each other by name all evening.

"Not at all." Brennan sent a glance across the puddled flagstones to the wooden stairs rising to the railed walk. There were lights, but of such thrifty wattage that there were stretches of dark. "Will you be all right?"

"Yes. Thank you again, and I'm sorry—" Unable to complete that, Mary shook her head, smiled, and walked rapidly to the rear entrance of the hotel, beside the bar. She said good-evening to the tireless Raoul, who was apparently in charge of parking problems in addition to all his other duties, and waited at the desk while the clerk addressed the telephone severely in Spanish; something, it seemed, to do with laundry.

He hung up. Yes, he told Mary, the young lady had picked up the key perhaps ten or fifteen minutes ago.

In her relief, uncalled-for though she knew it to be, Mary did not look beyond his faintly indulgent smile because Jenny aroused that kind of reaction. She went outside again to the courtyard sounds and sights blocked off before by her sense of urgency: occasional laughter over the syncopated thud of music from the bar, water running pink and gold among the flagstones, the black rain-ruffled droop of the willows around the swimming pool. The van that had blocked the entrance was gone, and Daniel

Brennan's car was presumably slotted away somewhere. She mounted the wooden steps, the shaky rail wet and surprisingly cold under her hand, and walked past a Stygian well housing some kind of machinery to the door of the corner room, and tapped.

"Jenny?"

No answer, not even a promising stir. If she had sealed herself into the shower, would she, in view of the time, have left the door unlocked although that was never the best of ideas?

The door opened under Mary's hand. The overhead light was on. A length of pink dress almost at her feet sent a terrible bounding through her chest, but Jenny wasn't inside it. She was under the covers in the nearest bed, face down, black hair every which way, oblivious.

She had come in a very short time ago, according to the desk clerk. She was almost crankily neat about hanging up her clothes. She had travelled down here with a calico nightgown that seemed to be her favorite, but only her bra strap showed on one bony bared shoulder. She was still wearing her costly pearls. She had ears like a deer, and she hadn't heard the opening or the closing of the door. Except for the very slight rise and fall of the blanket, she might have been dead.

"Jenny?" The fear at the pool might have been a rehearsal for this. Mary bent and placed the lightest of fingers on the exposed shoulder, forcing herself to speak calmly although there was something odd and wrong here. "Jenny? . . . *Jenny!*"

12

It took a frighteningly long time for the extravagant eyelashes to tremble and lift a little, reluctantly, on a flash of white and then dazed gray-blue before they dropped again. Jenny muttered indistinguishably and resumed her sleep. Mary straightened, astonished but relieved at the strong smell of liquor.

As simple as that, when for an uncountable number of heartbeats the room had seemed full of some unspecified danger. Jenny, acutely self-conscious about her hair and therefore doubly anxious to appear nonchalant and sophisticated to Owen St. Ives, had had drinks she wasn't used to and—if body weight had much to do with the assimilation of alcohol, couldn't tolerate. She would almost certainly have required assistance into the lobby for the key, as the clerk would scarcely turn it over to a strange man, and that was the cause of the understanding smile.

Here, Mary became aware that some of her relief was filtering away. Sitting on the other bed, gazing across at what little she could see of the profile between the long masking strands of hair, she thought uneasily that this looked somehow deeper than sleep, even liquor-induced sleep. Moreover, Owen St. Ives would have seen early what was happening to his young companion, and although there were people who found it entertaining to watch unsuspecting drinkers get drunk, and even fed liquor to parakeets or puppies, Mary was sure that he was not among them.

Sure? How? Because of some elusive quality of resemblance, she was going by the standards of another man entirely. She had even, although she had not recognized it until now, been deceiving herself into thinking that he felt a bond with her too as well as a compassison for Jenny.

Out of nowhere, chillingly, flashed a fact so taken for granted after a week's familiarity that it hadn't reminded her of its existence at once in this context. At least twice a day, possibly three times, Jenny took some kind of capsule.

What?

Briefly, Mary's skin seemed to blaze over the inner cold. There were medications so incompatible with alcohol—tranquilizers, usually, although why would marionette Jenny of all people be taking tranquilizers?—that the people who combined the two sometimes never woke up.

By this time she was at the other bed, shaking the sharp-angled shoulder, pushing back the disordered black hair. "Jenny. *Jenny.* Wake up. Can you hear me? Wake *up!*"

It was useless. Jenny's eyelids would lift a little at the insistent pressure of Mary's hands and then close again with no trace of any comprehension beyond her own need for oblivion, although once, patently to get rid of this interference, she mumbled "Okay," and burrowed her face deeper into the pillow.

There was no point in getting furious at her, and no point either in the self-recrimination at the other end of the pendulum. (You should have known she might do something like this. You knew she was besotted with Owen St. Ives, and you thought yourself that she looked like someone doing a little-girl impression.)

Above all, it would not help to give way to tears of worry and frustration in spite of a brand-new speculation which had slipped in on the heels of the other like an animal, not a domestic one, taking advantage of an opened door.

People who made an intensive study of the subject contended that a significant number of automobile fatalities could be considered to be suicides. Jenny had been courting danger at the pool. It was true that she had appeared to snap back to normal, but what if, in a short period of time, she had seen Brian Beardsley with Astrid in downtown Juarez and on top of that made the discovery that St. Ives liked her as an eighteen-year-old but nothing more?

You don't know that, Mary informed herself steadily. Jenny is not run-of-the-mill.

She went to the telephone and presently, watching

139

the unmoving, unhearing girl in the bed, got the Casa de Flores and asked for Owen St. Ives. He would certainly be able to tell her something— Jenny's mood, how much she had had to drink, whether she had taken one of her capsules. Almost from the first the ringing had a futile sound, but she let it go on long enough to penetrate the running of a shower before she hung up and stood for an indecisive moment with her hand on the receiver.

If she did call back with a message to phone this number, how likely was it that Owen St. Ives, returning, would stop at the desk and inquire? Or that the clerk would keep ringing his room faithfully?

For the first time, Mary was strengtheningly angry as well as alarmed. It was difficult to deflect Jenny from a chosen course, God knew, but by the very nature of things St. Ives would have more weight with her than anyone else. In view of her age and her current condition, he might have lingered here, at least briefly. Failing that, it should have been no insurmountable task to write a fast note: "Don't worry, Jenny's just had a drink too many."

Unless he hadn't realized—but of course he had. He would have seen Jenny up the difficult stairs and inside the room, and he would have known that she was only minutes away from passing out.

Mary left the telephone, studied her cousin again, hung up the pink dress as if it mattered to be tidy. Jenny's raincoat wasn't in the closet, it was on the bathroom floor with an air of having been aimed haphazardly at the door hook. Mary bent for it and felt in the pockets for a piece of paper thrust in bemusedly, but found only a leopard-printed chiffon scarf, a pair of gloves, and eleven cents.

The straw handbag was on the floor too. Mary zipped it open and combed rapidly through the contents for the small silver pillbox with a turquoise set in the lid which Jenny had bought in Santa Fe the day after her arrival ("Might as well be fancy about it"). It was empty, which told her nothing because she didn't know when it had last been filled from the mother lode in Jenny's suitcase.

Mary did not put the pocketbook down at once. Feeling that something important hinged on this, she made a thorough search for that other and actual note. It wasn't in the wastebasket, and Jenny could hardly have chewed it up and swallowed it, like a spy. And it was not an infringement of rights. In Santa Fe, she had heard a siren and assured herself that someone was in charge out there—but now she was in charge.

She found what she was looking for wedged into the thin folder of traveller's checks—for sentimental reasons, incredible though that seemed, or so that Jenny could remind herself that a man capable of this casual cruelty wasn't worth disrupting her life and alienating her parents for? It was a single line in a tight and punishing little hand: "How do you like my girl? Pretty, no?"

There was no signature, mockingly, but Jenny would know his writing. In view of her emaciation, it was like a kick at the head of someone who had stumbled and fallen, and all the more wounding because it was reasonable to believe that Astrid had shared in the fun. Mary thought back to her cousin's simple admiration of the other girl, felt like tearing the note into savage little pieces, put it scrupulously back instead.

. . . And how many moments lost here? Jenny was still deep in the sleep that might be natural under the circumstances or might be very dangerous indeed— was dangerous in any case, Mary realized suddenly, because it would be impossible to arouse her if necessary. This was an old building with a lot of wood, and if someone dozed off with a cigarette . . .

If she started thinking like this she would panic completely. Ask Daniel Brennan's advice before she tried to locate an English-speaking doctor and set events in train for which Jenny would probably never forgive her? He was right here at the hotel, and at some point he might have dealt, as Mary had not, with someone in this semicomatose condition; he might reassure her that it was simply a matter of sleeping it off.

Daniel Brennan was not in his room, and now her throat did begin to prickle.

Ask for the number of a doctor right now? But he would ask a few preliminary questions for which she should try to have intelligent answers, and Mary put the receiver back and went distractedly to feel the pulse in the wrist that might have been that of a young child. It was a ridiculous gesture, she knew as she made it: she had no idea of what a sleeper's pulse should be, let alone a drunken sleeper's, let alone a drunken sleeper's who couldn't be considered in normal health and had probably taken an unknown medication.

Still, Mary tried to assess the beat; it seemed light and far-spaced, but that might have been in contrast to her own speeded-up and violent pulse. She tucked Jenny's arm back and pulled the blanket higher, because the room wasn't warm, trying the usual talisman: someday I'll look back on this and wonder how I could have gotten so . . . But it didn't work, because she knew she would not forget this.

The suitcase, then, because once in a blue moon prescription labels contained actual information. There wasn't a tremor of awareness from Jenny at its thump on the neighboring bed, the sharp clicks from the catches. Mary pressed testingly on the contents in search of something hard and glassy, had to delve. A promising resistance inside one slipper proved to be cologne. She extricated the other slipper, and shook out a bottle nearly half-full of yellow-and-white capsules.

It was not one of the blue-moon instances. The label carried only Jenny's name and the doctor's, a date in March, and instructions to take one capsule three times daily.

There went the hope of an intelligent answer for a doctor. Fleetingly in a rage at Jenny and Dr. J. Wittenbaugh, and the Actons and Owen St. Ives and Daniel Brennan, Mary put the bottle back in its nest and yanked up folds of clothing to replace the slipper beside its mate.

Her uncaring fingers touched more than fabric and the daytime sandals parcelled out neatly at the sides of the suitcase. With a crackle electrifying in the silent room—Jenny a very concentration of stillness in her eerie sleep—a twist of newspaper, so tightly gathered as to have a recoil when it was nudged, flew free.

143

Another auxiliary bottle of capsules? No. A pair of pottery birds for salt and pepper, undoubtedly Jenny's house present for her. These were not gift-shop robins or canaries: the painted eyes were fierce and alert, the feathers a subtle gradation of slate-blue and mushroom and wheat-color under the high hard glaze. More carefully this time, Mary reached in to bundle the inevitable Mexican wrapping tight together again, and snatched her hand back and stared at her fingers.

Salt and pepper shakers did not come filled with anything, and this was in any case softer than salt, almost like powdered sugar with a faint suggestion of glisten. Mary did not taste it as detectives did in books, because she wouldn't have had any idea of what to expect and she felt that she didn't have to. This was cocaine or something like it. Buried at the bottom of a suitcase which in the normal course of events she would never have penetrated, introduced so hastily that one of the small bottom corks had not been pushed quite home.

An echo came back. Jenny, after they had been beckoned through Customs: "Can you get out again just as easily?"

Jenny, intimate of a known user.

But even if she had been so inclined—and she is *not*, said Mary steadily to herself—she would have had no knowledge of how to obtain the drug and no opportunity. Except for brief periods at the swimming pool, and the few requested minutes to shop alone and a fast foray for the morning newspaper at the Casa de Flores, she had been constantly with Mary.

144

In addition, this obvious cache, as opposed to the astonishing ingenuities cited in the newspapers, seemed meant to be found, had perhaps already been reported. As far as statistics were concerned, Jenny fell into the right age group and came from the East, where the street price for drugs was reportedly higher than in the Southwest, so close to the border.

The Mexican attitude toward Americans engaged in drug traffic within its boundaries was ferocious, and although there was now a treaty for prisoner exchange it would not, if it was like most governmental processes, be enacted with any particular speed in individual cases. The U.S. Embassy, if not quite taking a detached stance, was relatively powerless. Mary thought about what she had heard of Mexican prisons —and in fact listened to in scraps tonight at dinner; thought about Jenny in her vulnerable sleep, felt cold to her marrow.

Before a doctor, before anything, this terrifying white substance had to be disposed of, the pottery birds washed, the suitcase lining washed too. Because the newspaper wrapping had been so very tight, Mary didn't think that any of Jenny's clothes had been in contact with the drug, but she would have to make sure.

She had a desperate sense of haste, and her hands tended to shake. She lifted out garments, placed them to one side, carried the newspaper bundle carefully to the bathroom sink. She would flush away the cocaine, if that was what it was, and burn the wrappings later. And then she would—

Like a loud cry of warning, the telephone rang.

*   *   *

145

"I still think it was kind of a dirty trick," said Astrid pensively in the car driving north through the fringes of El Paso.

She had collected her promised due of dinner in a Juarez nightclub as a reward for her day's activities. First, the contrived meeting with Jenny Acton, then the hoped-for, almost predictable ride into town with her and Mary Vaughan: people who came to Mexico generally did shopping or sight-seeing. The instant taxi back to the Casa de Flores, where the clerk who had seen her in conversation with the two did not demur at all at giving her the key to her room when she said that she had left her wallet there.

The identification of the proper suitcase was as simple as she had been led to believe, and she hadn't even had to use the little lock-pick she had been given. The pottery birds were made to order, although it didn't really matter where she put the stuff, just so long as Jenny Acton wouldn't notice it at once. Then downstairs again, and the prepared envelope handed to the clerk with a winning smile: "I thought I'd explain to them in case we miss each other later on."

Brian Beardsley turned his head now and looked at her in the dim dashboard glow. "They lost me my job," he reminded her simply. "It'll teach them a lesson, that's all."

"But she won't really have to go to prison or anything, will she?" pursued Astrid.

She was younger than Mary Vaughan had thought, twenty, a college drop-out from North Carolina with a sense of values that shifted about like patterns in a kaleidoscope. As a beauty from the cradle on, she had been spared the tiny battles and skirmishings-for-position and despairing Saturday nights of most girls, and it might have been partly boredom that had led her to become involved with drugs in her freshman year. (She could easily uninvolve herself; she just hadn't wanted to yet.) Drifting to New York in the company of her roommate, she had encountered the incredible man at her side, and come willingly with him to Santa Fe and then Juarez.

Astrid had not seen any articles about Americans in Mexican jails for the simple reason that she never read newspapers: why distress herself with smolderings in the Middle East, earthquakes, politics, the chroniclings of children with leukemia? Still, into the oddly contemplative silence of the car, she repeated, "She won't really—"

"No problem," lied Brian Beardsley with calm. "Her people have money. They can get her out with a telephone call."

"Oh, good," said Astrid, who believed herself to be thinking quite rationally but was not, "because even though she's so skinny and all she seemed kind of nice. Well, I mean, you used to like her, didn't you?"

She would be a lot skinnier before long, thought Beardsley, and viewed with pleasure the powerful Actons coming humbly to a Juarez jail with food packages and perhaps medicines for their incarcerated daughter. He said indifferently, "She's not a bad kid."

And in fact for a time he had found Jenny different and interesting, a combination of cynic and believer in Santa Claus. His friends had looked upon her in the light of a mascot, and there had been a certain pride in the conquest—and there was, he discovered to his real surprise, the Acton money, unsuspected because of Jenny's casual and spent-looking wardrobe. He could do worse; he could do a whole lot worse.

The Actons had smiled reservedly on Jenny's announcement, and even—a declaration of upper-echelon war?—produced champagne in crystal glasses. Two weeks to the day, his employer had told him stiffly that they could scarcely have a man under investigation in the firm. His rage had been such that he had not made any attempt to see Jenny again but begun to ponder, instead, how he could pay these people back.

. . . As he had done, with his telephone call to the police just before he and Astrid left their motel; it seemed a good idea, on several counts, to be back over the border when they descended. He began to watch for the signs that would direct him west and eventually to California, where he knew a way to disappear for a while in case the Actons should think to point an accusing finger. It would be a pity in a way to divest himself of Astrid, but she was much too memorable and he had a friend who would like her.

And here she was, starting off about Jenny again: "Poor kid . . ." He turned on her with an intensity that made her cower against the seat. "How many times do I have to tell you that she'll be all right, for Christ's sake?" He grew calmer, with effort. "If you want somebody to feel sorry for, try me. I've got a four-hour drive to Nogales, while she's tucked up in her little bed . . ."

13

"Mary. I tried to call you a few minutes ago but your line was busy," said Owen St. Ives. "Tell me, how is Jenny?"

Mary closed her eyes and took a long breath, holding it for a few seconds out of sheer relief. "Asleep, or rather out cold. I've been frantic."

"But you saw my note."

"No, and I looked, and I couldn't—but I found . . ." This was near-incoherence; she must not babble. Into it, sharp as a flare of light, shot the memory of St. Ives in conversation with the chambermaid, the woman with the ready key. ". . . her doctor's telephone number, in New York. I was going to call him," said Mary. She steadied her fingers around the receiver, because she had arrived on safe ground. "Owen, what did Jenny have to drink?"

"A whiskey sour, which she must have sipped at for forty minutes, and a beer with dinner, which I thought at the time she had eaten most of," said St. Ives with a trace of grimness which Mary could understand: Jenny was an artist at concealing whole portions beneath a leaf of lettuce or a potato shell. "So far, so good. The people next to us were having brandy, and Jenny looked interested. By this time I had a notion that she wasn't used to drinking at all, but the waiter came up, they're good at this, and asked if we'd like a liqueur. I said I didn't think so but Jenny said yes, she'd like a brandy."

Mary turned her head and glanced at her cousin. It seemed somehow weird that they were discussing her in this detail and she wasn't hearing.

"Everything still seemed pretty much all right, until she spilled some of the brandy on herself," went on St. Ives. "It was—like lightning, I've never seen anything like it before, and she seemed as astonished as I was. I wish I'd had a clue."

It was a rueful comment; he was neither accusing nor defensive. Mary said honestly, "I didn't know either." For the first time it occurred to her that the evening must have been difficult for him. But she also thought that it wasn't such a staggering amount of liquor, taken over a period of time and with food, particularly as Jenny hadn't gotten to drink all of her brandy.

On the other hand, after that promising beginning at lunch, Jenny had consumed only half of her chicken sandwich and that had been a number of hours earlier. "Did she take a capsule, by any chance?"

"I think . . ." Small pause, in which Mary could picture a frown, followed by certainty. "Yes, I know she did, although she was very unobtrusive about it."

Again he was right; even with Mary, Jenny tended to use sleight-of-hand over this ritual. "She didn't— I'm sorry to keep asking you all these questions, but I'm worried about her—she didn't seem upset about anything, did she?"

"Not at all, she was enjoying herself right up until the fatal moment, or so she said. When I got her up to your room I tried to persuade her to vomit," said St. Ives sensibly, "but she wasn't interested in anything but going to sleep, so I just left you a note explaining what had happened so you wouldn't worry. I didn't dare lock her in, so I took a chance that you'd be back soon. I really don't think you have anything to be concerned about. She had all the classic symptoms—glazed eyes, cold sweat, the staggers —only speeded up, like a fast film. She must be one of those people who can't drink."

Mary hoped irrelevantly that Jenny would remember very little of all this; she did not need any more humiliations. She heard St. Ives say after another short pause, "Shall I come over and have a look at her? I've probably put more people to bed than you have."

"Oh, no," said Mary quickly, remembering the all-important task waiting for her in the bathroom basin. "I'll be fine, now that I know what happened."

She said goodnight, realizing after she had hung up that she hadn't thanked him for taking care of Jenny, realizing too that a part of her worry—the inability to get her cousin on her feet and moving if necessary —remained unsolved. She closed that thought off, because this was a time when she had to be very calm

151

and single-minded.

She flushed the white substance down the toilet, set a match to the newspapers in the sink with their powdery residue, washed the pottery birds although only one had been involved, washed the sink itself. Her hands were more reliable now, and she knew that it had been ridiculous to suspect St. Ives, however fleetingly, of this vicious thing. Even granted some reason for wanting to harm Jenny, and that was hard to grant, he had had all the opportunity in the world tonight. He would only have had to topple her casually into the swimming pool under the willows and go on his way; alcohol would have done the rest.

The answer had been there all along, from that moment of absolute certainty in the parking area at the Casa de Flores. It hadn't been enough for Brian Beardsley to show Jenny his succulent new girl while staying out of sight himself like a malicious child. By involving her with drugs he could really punish her, and her parents as well.

What would have happened if she hadn't disturbed the contents of Jenny's suitcase right down to the bottom? An informing telephone call leading to their apprehension, because with all that spite Brian Beardsley would surely have gotten the automobile license number from Astrid. Her and Jenny's insistence that they knew nothing about any cocaine; it had been planted there. (This must be a plea familiar to the point of boredom.) By whom had it been planted, did they think, and why?

It was within the bounds of possibility—but barely, thought Mary, remembering detailed and bitter newspaper accounts—that the Mexican police might

152

have tried to inquire locally about a Brian Beardsley, who would have taken the elementary precaution of registering under another name.

How fragile it would all sound anyway, particularly to the Latin temperament: these machinations so long after the fact, and especially when the man in question had a new and much prettier companion.

Astrid. Mary found her as hard to forgive as a poisoned apple. Looked back upon, she had picked them up as expertly as a man spotting a pretty girl in a bar. Badly run though the Casa de Flores was, she could not imagine them turning over the room key of two women to a strange man—but Astrid, visibly chatting with Jenny at the counter and then leaving the lobby with them, would be convincing. Plus the fact that she looked no more harmful than a ray of sunlight.

. . . The bottom of Jenny's suitcase appeared to be innocent, but what tests might they subject it to? Probably none, but it was better to be on the safe side. Mary wet the end of a towel, wrung it, heard with horror a brisk tap on the door.

Would they come at night like this? Of course they would; she could scarcely expect a solicitous call first. How was she going to explain the suitcase emptied on the bed? She thought she had seen a cockroach? A tarantula, an iguana? Would they accept her statement that Jenny's oblivion was the result of liquor and nothing else?

Mary walked to the door, determined to be militant (How dare you disturb me at this hour?), and opened it on Daniel Brennan.

* * *

Her reaction was so great that she simply stood there, staring at him, holding the doorknob as if it were a lifeline.

"They told me someone had called," said Brennan, "and as I don't know anyone else in the hotel I figured it could only be you and that you weren't calling just to say goodnight." His gaze slipped past Mary, towel forgotten in one hand, to the motionless girl in the bed and then the piled clothing beside the open suitcase. "Is Jenny—is everything all right?"

The pitch of a man's voice accomplished what Mary's urgings had not: Jenny gave a sudden enormous snore and was silent again. "Oh, everything's fine," said Mary, unbearably rebellious all at once at the battering her nerves had taken in the last half-hour, "except that Jenny's drunk and somebody put cocaine in her suitcase."

A beginning flicker at the corner of Brennan's mouth died at once. At the hollow sound of feet on the wooden stairs he stepped quickly inside the room, closing the door behind him as Mary's grip fell unresistingly away. He didn't waste time on incredulity. "What have you done with it?"

Mary told him. For just a second she thought bemusedly that this had happened before, and then she remembered that the other time it had been Owen St. Ives entering her room at the Casa de Flores. She said, "I don't know what they do in situations like this. Dogs . . . or is that only with marijuana? Anyway, I thought I ought to sponge the suitcase."

"It's not a bad idea. Here, I'll do it while you shake out the clothes," said Brennan. "Have you got any cologne?"

Mary gave him Jenny's, not asking whether this was for faster-drying purposes or to mislead any sniffers. In the mirror over the desk she caught a glimpse of Brennan's absorbed activities with the towel and her own housewifely gestures with Jenny's clothes, for all the world as if she were snapping laundry just off the line. Lurid scene in a Juarez hotel room, she thought, and didn't realize that she had given the beginning of an unstrung laugh until Brennan, straightening and discarding the towel, studied her and said abruptly, "What you need is a drink, in case you aren't aware of it. Let's put this stuff back and go down to the bar."

"But I've got a—" began Mary, and looked blankly around her: in her hasty packing she had left the Bacardi at the Casa de Flores. Instantly, the prospect of getting even briefly out of this room which at one point had seemed to close in on her, of sitting down with something long and mild and savoring her first cigarette since after dinner, was infinitely desirable.

And impossible. She said, "I can't leave Jenny."

"I don't know why not," said Brennan, practical. "She isn't going to miss you." He moved over to the other bed, said Jenny's name experimentally, bent to lift one of her eyelids and look at the returning pupil. He had a strangely professional air.

"Based on my unfortunately vast experience with a nephew who visits me in his cups, she's all right," he said, "and I can't imagine her waking up for at least a couple of hours. You're the one in need of attention." He glanced down again at the sleeping face, his own curious. "How on earth—?"

"She seems to have an allergic reaction to alcohol,"

155

said Mary. She located her handbag and, at the bathroom mirror, inspected her total pallor and commenced some swift repairs. There was no comment from beyond the door, but she made it to herself. Allergic—and unaware of it by age eighteen, living what could hardly be called a cloistered life? Or had she thought she could get away with it, just this once? Diabetics, long familiar with their condition, had been known to make rare, cautious departures from their regimes.

The brandy seemed ironic—she and Daniel Brennan with theirs, Owen St. Ives and Jenny sipping the same liqueur probably not far away. Her saying just now, "I can't leave Jenny," was a kind of echo of her insistence to St. Ives: "I've got to let Jenny know that I'm going." Almost like following steps in a shadow ballet.

Jenny stayed stubbornly at the heart of everything —but she was safe now that the pin had been pulled from Brian Beardsley's grenade and he was undoubtedly gone from Juarez.

There was hotel stationery in the desk, and although Daniel Brennan looked a little amused at this precaution Mary wrote, "Downstairs at the bar—have me paged there if you want me" and added the time and propped the sheet against the mirror, which was the first thing Jenny would see across the room if she opened her eyes and took in her surroundings.

(Where, incidentally, was the note which Owen St. Ives was so sure he had left for Mary, and which would have spared her those long minutes of near-panic? Why, for that matter, hadn't he said a firm,

156

"No, thanks," to that interfering waiter, or even overridden Jenny's request for brandy? She was smitten with him, and would have been obedient.)

"You keep going away," observed Brennan pleasantly, holding the coat which Mary had picked up distractedly.

"Yes, I know. I'm sorry." Another echo, thought Mary as she put her arms into the coat. She had said the same thing to him not an hour ago, and to Owen St. Ives when a necessitous feeling had driven her out of his car. She picked up the key from the desk, and said doubtfully, "Do we lock the door?"

"We certainly do." Brennan was forceful about it, although this was the kind of mechanism which would leave Jenny imprisoned. "Jaime's is a nice place, but there odd people everywhere."

The night was chilly, holding left-over drips and glistens from the rain. Brennan was giving off little whiffs of Jenny's cologne as he moved, but luckily he seemed unaware of this. Halfway to the stairs along the railed walk, a door came a few inches open at the sound of their footsteps, and a man's voice called jovially, "Hey, what kept you so long?" He could only have seen the dimmest of outlines against the sporadically lighted front of the far side of the annex, but he said at once, "Oh, I beg your pardon," and closed the door.

"We had a few things to clean up," murmured Brennan.

He went before Mary down the steps, and strolled across to the edge of the willow-sheltered pool, which, not lit, held only little tremors of reflected pinkish-gold on its dark surface, along with a faint brilliance, at the shallow end, from a lamp at a corner of the building. "Someone dropped either a silver dollar or a pendant in here this afternoon," he said conversationally. "I wonder if it's been retrieved? I told one of the bus boys about it."

Not caring much, Mary joined him automatically. There was always something fascinating about water, particularly in a dry country and perhaps especially at night. Any daytime gaiety had been swallowed up then, with the depths renewing their cold secrets until sunlight wiped them clear again.

She looked at a faint half-curve of glitter on the bottom, at perhaps four feet, and pointed. "There it is."

Brennan moved closer. "Well, I suppose it can't go down the drain," he said, and turned to glance curiously at her through the obscurity. "I didn't do a very good job of explaining myself at dinner. What I really meant to say—"

Something brushed lightly between Mary's shoulder-blades. It was only, could only have been a frond of willow, but she stepped instantly away. She didn't want to hear what he had meant to say, not just now, even though there have been a peculiar intimacy in the room where they had worked while Jenny slept. She had a slight sense of dizziness, as if the metallic curve on the pool bottom were a shining object suspended by a hypnotist.

"You're cold," said Brennan abruptly as shafts of willow-fragmented gold struck across at them and a car engine started. In the same unobtrusive way in which he had claimed the doorknob upstairs, he now had possession of Mary's elbow. "Let's get that drink."

She hadn't been aware until then of a physical chill, but in the bar she gave a reminiscent shiver. Mercifully, the musicians had departed. As at the motel pool, Brennan did not rely on the mercies of a waiter, but went off and returned speedily with their drinks.

He didn't pick up where he had left off outside. He asked instead, "Who do you think was responsible for the sabotage?"

Which he had accepted at once, even though he viewed Jenny with a fairly cool eye; that fact was suddenly as warming as the drink. "The man I told you about at dinner, the one with Astrid," said Mary. Without realizing it, she must have been preparing a cut version of this. "Jenny was quite involved with him a couple of months ago, and he was furious when she broke it off. He isn't, I gather, a man who likes being crossed."

"Unlike the rest of us who revel in it," remarked Brennan, giving her a mildly amused look. "He was certainly going to get his revenge, with bells on, but how did he . . . ? Oh, Astrid, I suppose, as she was staying right there with her nonexistent aunt and uncle. Lucky you found the stuff in time."

He hadn't, naturally, commented on her motives for exploring Jenny's suitcase in the first place—but then for all he knew Mary was a chronic opener of other people's mail, a listener at keyholes, a reader of diaries not her own. She said with firmness, "Yes, it was. If I hadn't gotten worried about the com-

159

bination of liquor and whatever prescription Jenny takes . . ."

"It's none of my business, I know," said Brennan into the little trail-away silence, "but Jenny looks as though a Shirley Temple would set her on her ear. Who let her—?"

Mary supposed that it was his business, in a fringe way, because he had helped her unquestioningly. Still, the implied criticism—just as if she had not framed a related wonder to herself—made her prickle slightly.

"Another guest at the motel, who must have been as startled at what happened as I was." How to undo the impression of two lone females in Mexico on pleasure bent, dividing up for a little adventure: that one's mine, you can have the other? To explain that she was to have been a member of that party would suggest either that good manners in honoring Brennan's prior invitation had spoiled her evening or that she had preferred his company.

Mary finished her cigarette without hurry, to avoid any appearance of even minor confusion, and slipped her coat back on. "I'm sure Jenny's still in the depths, but I think I ought to be back there anyway. Thank you for the drink, and for your help upstairs—I was on the point of flying to pieces."

"You were keeping your head very well." Brennan was standing too, gesturing down at her glass, still a third full. "But you haven't—"

"I've had enough to restore me, honestly," said Mary, and said goodnight and departed. She hoped as she crossed the courtyard that there were extra blankets in the room; the temperature seemed to have dropped a few degrees in the last half-hour, and there was obviously a late-spring storm on the way.

What had begun as an excuse to Daniel Brennan was suddenly true. Jenny certainly hadn't looked like waking for some time, but her physical reactions were unpredictable. She could have received only the blurriest of impressions of the room to which Owen St. Ives had delivered her, so that she would open her eyes to what in effect were strange surroundings. She might even try the door before she discovered that propped-up piece of paper to be a note—it wasn't likely that she would regain consciousness with a mind as clear as a bell—and find herself locked in.

Mary, who was mildly claustrophobic and would hate such a circumstance, quickened her steps on the wooden stairs. It crossed her mind that this audibly hurrying pace would have drawn a sharper vigilance than ever from those odd inhabitants at the Casa de Flores.

The stingy light at the top of the stairs receded as she passed the three intervening rooms to the corner one, key in her hand. She whirled and nearly dropped it as the black shadows against the wall broke and a man said her name.

14

For a shaken second, Mary thought that Owen St. Ives was going to pull her into his arms, key and all. Then he said simply, "Thank God. I called back a little while after I talked to you, and when there was no answer—May I come in for a minute?"

"Of course. I was only downstairs," said Mary, having a little unaccountable trouble with the key. She got the door open and went instantly to examine Jenny, who had shifted position and was lying on her other side, her hair a fresh tangle of black. Her breathing seemed even and unchanged.

"You can see why I was so worried until I talked to you," said Mary, turning to St. Ives. He must have waited outside for quite a while, she thought as he closed the door; two fingers on his right hand were almost white with cold. He nodded at her, pushing both hands into his pockets as though self-conscious about this frailty—Mary's own ungloved hands had

162

felt chilly, but not to that extent—and joined her at the bedside, gazing down with an abstracted frown.

"I was feeling badly about Jenny," he said in a troubled voice, "and I started analyzing it and wondering if it *was* the drinks that knocked her out? She stretched her cocktail to last through two of mine, and she did at least eat part of her dinner. And then when I called back, and there was no one here, I was afraid it might have been something else, that she might have gotten worse. I couldn't find your car anywhere, and I thought you might have gone for a doctor, or—God knows what I thought."

"My car wouldn't start, it's still at the motel." Mary was finding his apprehension about Jenny's condition difficult to follow. Food poisoning wasn't unheard of in Mexico, but it did not send one into a profound sleep, to put it mildly. "What do you mean by something else?"

St. Ives didn't answer that. Instead, he asked abuptly, "Do you know a David Brand in Santa Fe?"

It didn't ring the faintest of bells, and Mary shook her head. Her legs felt tired or unreliable or in some way unwilling to keep on holding her up. She dropped down on one of the inhospitable chairs, inviting St. Ives wordlessly to take the other, but he stood there beside Jenny, a core of restlessness even though he was still. He said, "I asked Jenny, tonight, who you'd gone out with, and she said someone named Daniel Brennan, who had apparently remembered you from Santa Fe."

A quiet fist seemed to close over Mary's breathing because of his tone. She said, astonishing herself, "Yes, he thought he had, but it turned out to be

163

someone else he had in mind."

"I saw him last night in the lobby," said St. Ives steadily, "and I recognized him from a village meeting in Albuquerque about two months ago. Very few people came out for it because there was a storm, and I couldn't have been mistaken. I started across to him to say hello, and he saw me coming and walked out the door."

A child would have grasped the implication. David Brand, Daniel Brennan—either initialled luggage or the psychological factor. "Daniel Brennan lives in Santa Fe," said Mary, equally steady. "He owns part of a shop there."

Owen St. Ives commented on that only with his eyebrows. "Did you get an El Paso newspaper tonight by any chance?"

"No."

"David Brand's wife was attacked and killed in Santa Fe the night before last," said St. Ives, and now he did change his mind and sit down in the other hard and armless chair.

Echoes, Mary had thought before—but this seemed more like a gradual and dangerous quickening of drums. "No worse, you must admit, than those women's shops where . . ." "You know about those." "Yes." Single syllable, shutting off any further light discussion. She remembered those comical little whiffs of cologne, and felt sick. She said, as one who knew, "The world is full of people who resemble other people, and a man whose wife had just been killed in Santa Fe wouldn't be here in Juarez."

"Yes, I know, I thought the same thing." The dark blue gaze was puzzled. "But I'm certain he's Brand,

164

and people react differently to shock." St. Ives turned his head and studied the bed with its oblivious occupant. "Jenny told me that he had dived in after her at the pool this afternoon, and that in fact he'd been there for some time."

"Yes, he'd been working at the motel with a buyer . . ." But would a man who had just lost his wife by violence have been carrying on business as usual? Or would he, while the onlooking attention was rivetted on Jenny's diving, have seized the opportunity to extract the silver pillbox from the handily unzipped bag, sauntered off to the passageway with it, substituted something else for the contents of one of the capsules?

Judging by the number of overdose victims, sleeping pills couldn't be hard to come by. Or borrow. No friend would think it odd under the circumstances if a man said, "Could you let me have something . . ." Because this was what St. Ives was clearly aiming at: Brennan's presence on the scene, Jenny's startling collapse later.

Oh, this is mad, thought Mary angrily. She said, "All right, suppose he is this David Brand. Jenny and I still met him for the first time last night, and we certainly had no connection with his wife.

St. Ives starred at her with the kind of brilliance which indicates thoughts turned inward. "Unless," he said slowly, "you happen to resemble her."

Late, late movie, thought Mary, trying protectively to reduce it to theatrical nonsense. Sudden widower crazed with grief, finding it unendurable that someone who looked like his wife was walking

165

around in perfect health. (That initial attention from across a dining room, fastening on her like an actual touch.) Immobilizing the look-alike's companion, so that he could destroy her without immediate hue or cry.

Which Daniel Brennan could have done quite easily an hour ago, if he had wanted to, with Jenny in her comatose state.

Leaving his fingerprints more or less all over the room? How quiet the pool, on the other hand. Simply from dinner, with drinks and brandy, her blood would have a certain alcohol content, and who could say with certainty how much it took to render someone helpless in the water? "She saw this silver thing on the bottom of the pool, and before I could stop her—"

But why say anything at all? Until the headlights came snapping on they been an unidentifiable man and woman in near-darkness, just as they had been in the car on the way to the restaurant—and then there had been that fierce rush of light and glancing impact. The woman in the rain hat had seen and talked to Mary . . .

She pressed a hand against her forehead like someone trying to extinguish a fever. She had thought, and rightly, that Jenny was a target here, and nothing would shake her conviction that the cocaine was the doing of Brian Beardsley, the known user of drugs. But what if, out of a nightmarish conjunction of circumstances, she had been a target too, and not only of an abiding malice?

Somehow included in her tumbling brain was the recollection that Spence had been almost chillingly

166

accurate in his assessment of people. Frequently, when Mary met someone likable and diverting at a party, he would ask later in amazement, "You didn't really believe a word of all that claptrap, did you?" and nine times out of then he would be right.

But this was St. Ives, now saying, "Maybe I'm wrong. People do strange things under stress, and maybe Brand is using another name because he thinks taking off for Juarez right after his wife was killed would look peculiar. Maybe there's nothing wrong with Jenny that a few hours' sleep won't cure. But—" he glanced at the bed "—I'm the responsible party, I'm the one who took her out, and I'd feel a lot better if we got her to a doctor."

"Daniel Brennan thought she looked—" began Mary involuntarily, and stopped short. He had come to the room to satisfy himself that Jenny would not be awake and aware for some time, and of course he would say there was nothing to worry about. She glanced at her own message for Jenny, still propped in position. It made no mention of Brennan.

Owen St. Ives had turned a shocked face. When Mary explained, very briefly because of her increasing sense of the need to hurry, he seemed less appalled by the planting of the drug than by the fact that the other man had actually been here. He said decisively, "Well, Brand isn't a doctor, that I do know, and I doubt very much that we'll get one to come here at this hour . . . Let's see if we can get her dressed."

As if her name had been called, Jenny gave a smothered, cut-off snore. Mary had found this comforting earlier, as a normal sound emanating from

167

deep sleep; now she wondered if it could be a sub-conscious cry for help. She went to the closet and took out the pink dress, its hanger clattering against the next under her shaky fingers. "But the stairs—we'll never manage . . ."

"There's a service elevator, I saw it while I was waiting for you," said St. Ives, giving an indicative nod in the direction of the dark well. He walked to the phone, picked up the receiver, put it down again. "Jenny isn't going to like having this noised about," he said, "and the hospital will certainly have an emergency room. Or—what do you think?"

"I think we should just go," said Mary, already beginning to feel as if she had been running, "but you're going to have to help me sit her up."

Jenny would have burned with humiliation if aware that all her ribs were on display and easily countable between her bra and half-slip. As it was, she only lifted her eyelids as St. Ives' propping arm went around her shoulders, gave them a glazed and uncomprehending look, muttered something about parakeets.

"It's all right, Jenny," said Mary soothingly as she maneuvered an arm into a sleeve. "We're just going to—" She broke off as St. Ives reminded her with a mute head-shake that Jenny had undoubtedly had her fill of doctors and might set up some kind of instinctive rebellion. She wasn't helping, at the moment, but neither was she resisting. It was like dressing a very large doll.

Here was one of her shoes, lying on its side at the foot of the bed. Some mixed-up monitor in Jenny's head must have instructed her to turn back the bedspread, as if for a fully dressed daytime nap, because the other shoe was underneath it. So was St. Ives' message, now somewhat crumpled: "Mary—Jenny didn't really have this much to drink but she has *no* head for liquor." The underscoring was so pronounced that if Mary had found the note at once she might have been reassured enough to go peacefully to sleep, while in the next bed—

But she spoke to us just now, thought Mary, blanking out a frightful vision of waking to find Jenny stilled forever. It was nonsense, but she spoke.

"Where's her coat?" asked St. Ives urgently, and Mary brought it from the bathroom. Together, while Jenny's head lolled, they got her arms into the sleeves and managed her upright and to the door. Surprisingly, her legs moved like the wheels of a mechanical toy in need of oiling, late but obedient. It wouldn't matter for her sake if anyone saw her being conducted along in this head-hanging fashion, because Mary was certain that it would be safe to leave here in the morning.

But was Daniel Brennan watching from somewhere, right now?

Brennan was not. He had finished his drink and ordered another, not that he particularly wanted it but because his room and his bed, one of Jaime's creakily protesting specials, had no immediate appeal. Also, the evening had gone as empty as a bottle upended over a sink.

A guest at the motel, Mary Vaughan had said to his inquiry about Jenny's dinner companion, and she had sounded defensive. She did not want the man criticized—unless it was some motherly woman, which Brennan doubted very much. In spite of her skin-and-bone appearance, Jenny had a core of strength—and physical strength as well, as who should know better than he after her fierce and wiry resistance in the pool?—which he suspected other women would recognize.

He should have clarified himself to Mary Vaughan (or Mary, he said tentatively to himself), previous and even egregious though it had seemed at the time. It was clear in every line of her that she was not a dallier with married men and for all she knew he had an unsuspecting wife and possibly a few children at home. But—even though she had looked to him across a lobby and then a dining room like the piece of incredible good fortune that doesn't drop into a man's life more than once—how to say, with the proper casualness, "I was married four years ago, or I thought I was until husband number one turned out to be hale, well, and undivorced"?

Mina. Black-haired, gray-eyed, captivating him with the diverse activities—ballet lessons, a course in Greek and another in gourmet cooking—which had turned out to be not evidence of a lively mind and energy but a dissatisfaction that burned like an eternal flame. Unfairly, she had turned him against women of that particular coloring, like Jenny Acton.

Who had an enemy, which automatically involved her travelling companion. Was the planting of a drug the entire gratification of revenge, retaliation, whatever it was? Brennan supposed so; it certainly seemed enough. Still, he wished that Mary had left

170

her lighter or cigarettes behind, so that he could go legitimately back to her door and see for himself that all was well.

There was no need to talk deceptively inside his own head. Of course all was well, although from the looks of her Jenny was assembling a hangover measurable on the Richter scale. He simply wanted to see Mary again before he slept. He could and would look her up in Santa Fe, but her life was probably full of people, and at any remove from the immediacy of her situation this evening he would be only an unwelcome reminder of a very unpleasant episode. Gloomily, he could hear her saying to some unspecified person, "If a Mr. Brennan calls, I'm not in."

In spite of its location and appearance, Jaime's was not a nest of revellers, and at a little after eleven-thirty the bar was beginning to empty, most of its inhabitants trailing off in the direction of the lobby and stairs, a few causing the slamming of car doors and starting of engines in the courtyard. Brennan wasn't sleepy, thought of the thin blear of light from the lamp over his bed and remembered the hundred-watt bulb, bought that morning, reposing in the glove compartment of his car. He finished his drink and went outside.

A few windows were still lit, but the unseasonable chill had chased most of the guests in and to bed early. Mary's upstairs corner room, to which his gaze lifted at once, was dark. Her hazel eyes had looked brilliant with fatigue; she must have gone to sleep almost at once.

Would she be roused by a sharp police knocking?

171

Probably, if she had left this address behind her at the Casa de Flores, although he couldn't imagine why she would. Jenny's ex-gentleman friend would have directed the police to the motel, with a tale of having been approached with cocaine for sale, but how far did they go when their bird had flown? Make an automatic check of other motels, in case Jenny Acton had taken alarm and moved out?

Or simply notify U.S. Customs, with the rider that this drug-peddler belonged in Mexican jurisdiction because the event in question had taken place on their soil?

Brennan had no idea. It hardly mattered, because the suitcase was thoroughly clean, apart from the worrying notion of Mary being waked and subjected to even a brief interrogation. Obviously they couldn't ask questions of Jenny.

A car came around the corner of the annex as Brennan unlocked the door of his and reached into the glove department. A departing employee, because that was the service area.

But, although it wasn't unusual for their U.S. counterparts to own something something startling in the way of transportation, Mexican waiters and bus boys did not drive cars of this newness and polish. Jaime himself, if there actually was such a man? Light bulb in hand, Brennan turned for a curious look.

Star-shaped red tail-lights, the front seats of the car poised briefly at the gate the tall tapering kind suggesting a pair of nuns. There were two occupants; the interior light flicked briefly on and showed a dipping profile as the passenger door was opened a little—for a fold of caught clothing?—and closed again.

Somehow astonishingly, because it meant that she had left Jenny behind her in a dark room, Mary Vaughan.

15

In the back seat, after an inarticulate mumble of protest when for all St. Ives' care her head got bumped smartly, Jenny had subsided into a tangle of hair and raincoat and Raggedy Ann legs. Her disorientation seemed complete. She had opened her eyes once in the shadowy service area where Mary held her propped while Owen St. Ives went for his car, but showed neither surprise nor concern at these peculiar surroundings.

It was only what amounted to black-out, wasn't it? They would know very shortly. At St. Ives' suggestion, Mary had pocketed one of the yellow-and-white capsules from Jenny's suitcase, because while medications came in all kinds of color combinations, depending on the manufacturer, it was just possible that a doctor might be able to identify this one at once.

The trip from the room to the service elevator and

174

then down had been accomplished without incident —without, in fact, meeting another soul, a fact for which Mary was grateful; she found that an innocent and necessitous act bestowed a feeling of near-criminality when carried out with every appearance of stealth. Jenny's condition would be evident to a closer look and a sniff, but at first glance she would be put down as the victim of kidnapers.

Mary had expected some kind of investigation when the elevator doors rattled open—for service only, this mechanism did not seem to get a lot of smooth care—and again when St. Ives used the rear exit to go out for his car. But at this hour a kitchen crew was loudly busy, behind heavy swing doors, with dishes, pots and pans, pails, occasional shouted sallies and less genial imprecations.

She felt calmer now that they were actually on their way to the hospital, but still with a nervous need to talk. "*This* would have caused a fluster at the Casa de Flores," she said as they turned out through the gate, and then, "I didn't want to alarm Jenny yesterday, but I'm almost sure I did hear something odd from that room last night."

". . . So did I," said St. Ives, giving her his belated attention. Downtown Juarez had by no means gone to bed, and he was having to be forceful about maintaining his place in the thick stream of lights. Bicycles wanted to cut in; so did taxis. "I found out tonight that the invalid, or whatever he is, was evidently in a state where the nurse decided that some female company would calm him down, so one of the prettier bar waitresses was sent up."

He sounded the horn lightly at the car in front,

175

whose driver was engaged in conversation with a companion although the red light had turned green. "The girl is no longer at the motel—handsomely paid off, I assume, and with a recommendation somewhere else—but she's a cousin of the room-service waiter I talked to originally and she told him that the man sprang at her, babbling about company spies, and blacked her eye before the nurse, and a hefty one at that, could get him under control. He wasn't young," added St. Ives.

A proxy fight had been one of his earlier speculations, Mary remembered, wincing a little at the speed with which the girl had been sent up as an offering. Had the man then begun to believe, because a notion once entertained in an unbalanced mind was apt to send out tendrils everywhere, that she and Jenny were also spies? That sudden heavy impact against the door behind her chair, as though to crash through it . . . Did he only have bouts of this, had he been spirited off to Mexico by one faction so that he should not be viewed in his current state by another?

The hospital would be coming up soon on their left, and like a number of smokers Mary was increasingly careful about lighting a cigarette in places where it would be considered offensive, even though this new campaign placed a weapon in the hands of uncaring people who had never had a weapon before and tended to use it with zeal. She reached inside her bag for package and lighter. "I suppose we'll never know, exactly."

"I suppose not," agreed St. Ives. He sounded faintly amused—at something he was discreetly keeping back about the bar waitress?

Although the traffic was thinning, he was keeping an eye on the rear-view mirror, and he wrenched the car suddenly into a side street. "Gang of toughs behind us, waving bottles," he said. "I'd just as soon lose them for a couple of minutes."

"I think that was the hospital, up ahead in the next block," said Mary, having had a fast glimpse of a modernistic building with blue lights to mark it. But it was too late; they would have to circle back. The front entrance had looked peculiarly closed for the night, but that couldn't be so. Sirens sounded frequently in the city during the small hours, and at least some of them must indicate victims of traffic accident or violent family argument.

Had there been a small Pavlovian stir from Jenny at the word "hospital"?

Mary twisted to peer back between the difficult seats, but they were off the main street now and it was too dark to see anything but a vague sprawl and a pale glimmer of face. Because of that brief inspection, she was late in registering the direction they had taken, right instead of the expected left, although surely they had shaken off that car with youths in a trouble-making mood?

They had run out of shops quite a while ago, and now out of small, close-packed houses. This was an area of trees on one side, and what looked like the laying out of an industrial complex on the other; there were cordoned-off stretches of cement, some skeletal framework, piled bricks. Beyond, the headlights picked out a crumbling adobe building, its sides studded decoratively with the bottoms of thrust-in-green glass bottles, and St. Ives was pulling the car up in front of it.

Mary gazed expectantly at him, waiting for him to back and turn, said bewilderedly when he made no motion toward doing so, "What are we—? To get to the hospital we have to—"

"We aren't going to any goddamned hospital," said St. Ives in a voice like an exposed knife-blade. "We never were."

For seconds, while the car gave off the tiny sounds that follow a suddenly switched-off ignition, Mary thought that she must have misheard him. She hadn't. She realized with a hard heavy beating in her throat that this terrible slippage, this abrupt canting of everything in sight which must be experienced by stroke-sufferers, was happening.

She put out a hand instinctively to the door handle, remembered Jenny helpless in the back seat with her dreams of parakeets, withdrew it again. She heard herself say steadily, like someone pretending fearlessness to a dog with its lips drawn back and its hair up, "I don't understand this, Owen." *Speak to it by name.* "Why are we here?"

"Why are we here?" mimicked the man who called himself Owen St. Ives. There was the worst kind of mockery in it, as though Mary had been making flirtatious advances. "So that I can kill you," he said, "like you killed my wife."

Even over the pounding of her blood, Mary felt a certain relief, because out of her own indisputable innocence she could argue with him, ultimately con-

178

vince him. She could account for herself on the night before last, because this had to be what it was all about; give him the names of the two men she had been with at a long dinner, assure him that Jenny could back her up about the quiet evening after-wards.

"If you're David Brand—" she said out of a pinched throat.

He gave a sharp bark which wasn't laughter but a release of hoarded-up hatred. It was as horrifying as seeing a cloth snatched away from apparently healthy flesh to reveal an abcess at bursting point. "I liked the initials. Go on, you murdering bitch."

"I'm sorry about what happened to your wife, but I swear that I never even met her," said Mary, dis-covering that it was possible even now to flinch at that invective in that particular voice. (But how would you know if you'd met her, whirled through her brain, when his name isn't even Brand?) "I've never harmed anyone, that I know of, in my life. I've certainly never—"

"You thought she was too far gone to describe you after you turned her away from your door, didn't you?" said the man facing her. "Oh, but she wasn't. She told me about the wagon-wheel in your gate, where she nearly fell down, and your blonde hair—" mincingly, terrifyingly, the silhouetted fingers flick-ered about his head, and he could never have thought that up by himself, he was copying a woman's gesture "—and the light you turned out in her face. Do you know how long she ran, bleeding?"

Mary's stomach turned over with foreknowledge. The subdued lights in the living room when she got

179

back. Jenny's shower cap, pale yellow, frilly, looking like hair to a desperate woman outside in the dark. Jenny's almost pathological squeamishness at the sight of blood, her anxiety to see a newspaper the next morning, her momentary terror when a strange woman had stalked toward her with apparent intention at the Casa de Flores. Like someone washed free of blood, and coming back to make her pay?

But Jenny lay in the back seat, unable to protect herself.

"All right, I was frightened," said Mary, trying in her horror to follow what must have been sleeping Jenny's course. "There had been some break-ins in my neighborhood, with violence, and I didn't dare open the door. And then I heard an ambulance a few minutes later, and I was sure that whoever it was had been rescued. In fact, I heard *two* sirens, so I—"

Swiftly, without warning, her throat was encircled. It might almost have been a lover's caress, except for the hovering thumbs. "Beg me," said the man pleasantly.

Mary's throat closed on an obedient *Please*. This was what he wanted, this was to be the aperitif, this was why she had been spared in the corridor on that first evening when the door at the far end had opened and those watchful eyes looked out. And if she had gone with him on that purported shopping errand? She hadn't been seen leaving with him, so that no one, later, could have said how she had come to be dead, strangled, in an abandoned adobe building.

Except that someone in the restaurant or the bar might have remembered her with Daniel Brennan,

180

and the woman in the rain hat, if she were still here at the time, would come forward. And as a witness—but Mary didn't see how he could leave her to be a witness—Jenny would be no good at all.

"I told Daniel Brennan you'd taken Jenny out to dinner," said Mary, finding a level for her voice although the thumbs had come down lightly, testingly, prolongingly—and, oh, God, why hadn't she? "If anything happens to me, after what happened to her, they'll look for you."

And what satisfaction in that, when she was dead and a certain number of people sent flowers and went to her grave, saying soberly among themselves that at least the police had her killer? Who might, in view of his wife's fate, get a reasonably light term. Uttering bad checks in New Mexico was a matter of extreme gravity; murder was frequently lesser.

Although the car was not designed for kicking, Mary tried it wildly, and was rewarded by a further pressure on her neck. She and Jenny wouldn't be here with this deadly presence if she had had the wit to analyze what he had given as an explanation for his anxiety while he waited for her in the shadows outside her room: "I couldn't find your car anywhere."

But at no time had he seen her in it, so he couldn't have identified it unless he had followed it from Santa Fe in his blue one, and disabled it to insure her presence in Juarez through tonight.

"How does it feel now?" asked St. Ives curiously, leaning back from the desperately reaching hands that felt attached to arms of cotton. "How do you like it, Mary Vaughan?"

181

The pain in her lungs, the outrage from her heart, were intolerable. At the moment he didn't really care what happened to him, thought Mary dimmingly; he was obsessed. Her brain seemed to flicker like a light bulb about to fail, and there was an eruption from the back seat and the terrible grip loosened and then fell away from her throat.

Jenny, swimming, tennis-playing Jenny, had an arm tight around the neck of the man in front of her, her wrist locked in her other hand, so that his head was tilted sharply back. She was crying in a broken and frantic way, as if she had been bottling up sobs for minutes, but she managed to say, "Oh, run, quick!"

And leave Jenny here with him, now that she had turned from simple cargo into a witness? She had to. To run, screaming, was the only hope for them both, because St. Ives had commenced a grim thrashing. How many more seconds could Jenny hold on, wiry though she was?

Still gasping, her throat feeling lined with briars, Mary stumbled out into the road, nearly fell, steadied herself in dimness; in order to see what he was doing, in this dark deserted place, St. Ives had left his parking lights on.

They snapped off as Mary began to run. He might be—he *had* to be—still imprisoned in that armlock, but he had remembered that. She screamed, frightening herself further, thinking with despair that it was like lighting a match in a vast black cellar, and a pair of cars came careening around the corner. The second one was a police car, its roof-light wheeling furiously.

Daniel Brennan whipped his door open and caught Mary as she staggered against his fender. His headlights were on full, and they reflected off two dull red star-shapes down the road. She gasped, "Jenny," pointing, and without a word he raced toward them. Two brown-uniformed policemen pelted after him, shouting in Spanish; one of them drew his gun.

Oh, God, they'll shoot him, thought Mary drearily. The road came up to meet her, but so gradually that it didn't even hurt.

At the police station, there was a buzz of excitement when, along with Brennan and St. Ives, Mary and Jenny gave their names and their address in Juarez. A fast order was issued, and a man departed at speed. Mary did not risk a glance at Brennan, because the police did not appear particularly friendly, but heard him give a small recognizing cough.

He had already paid severe fines for speeding and running a red light in the course of following St. Ives' car with its glowing stars. When stopped, and in the erroneous belief that Mary was somehow compulsively in the company of the drug-planter, he had managed to convince the police that there was someone in danger in the car he was pursuing. St. Ives had surprised him with that sudden unsignalled turn, and with the pattern of one-way streets and the police on his tail, he had had to go around two blocks.

St. Ives was handcuffed because he had resisted the police, but in spite of that, to Mary, he did not look particularly safe. Now that he no longer had to maintain a pose, the very cast of his features had altered, and it seemed impossible that he had ever smiled at her, speculated lightly on the invisible man at the Casa de Flores, given her what he had discovered as they drove—to divert her attention as he prepared to swing away from the hospital? His eyes were terrifying.

Although her tongue slipped and slurred occasionally, Jenny was shakily sober. She had told Mary and Daniel Brennan on the way to the police station in his car, closely shepherded by the police with St. Ives, that her whiskey sour before dinner had tasted bitter, but she didn't know what to expect of a whiskey sour and she had drunk it. Yes, she had been away from the table once when St. Ives told her smilingly that she had a smudge on her cheek, although, when she got to the ladies' room, she hadn't.

It was the pain from the bump to her head upon being bundled into the car—intentional, it might be supposed, as further insurance that she stay incapacitated—which had begun to penetrate the fog of a double dose of tranquilizers with unaccustomed alcohol on top. She had heard the mention of a hospital, which had spurred the wakening process, and then the frightful accusation leveled against Mary.

Now, under the bald lights and the suspicious stares of the police because she still gave off an aroma of brandy, Jenny said across the room to St. Ives, "It wasn't Mary, it was me," and, as he gave a contemptuous stir, "I had a yellow shower cap on."

The police gazes narrowed with incredulity and tennis-match attention. They were allowing this, Mary was sure, because they were waiting for the

184

report on the luggage searched at Jaime's Hotel.

"I thought it was a man—she had such short hair and she was wearing a man's shirt, and I really couldn't see her face because—" Jenny ducked her head, shying away from that, raised it again with courage. "I thought that whoever could beat up a man so badly might be coming after him, trying to get into the house too, and I was all alone and I—"

She didn't finish that, probably couldn't finish it even to herself for a long time. But, Mary realized with astonishment and admiration, in spite of what must have been her extreme shock when St. Ives changed character before her eyes, she was being deliberately elliptical for the police. She was pointing a way, so that they mightn't all be detained here forever.

"I did think," said Jenny steadily to the man she had fallen at least a little in love with, "that everything was all right when I heard an ambulance just a few minutes later."

The effect on St. Ives was peculiar. Mary saw the moment when he believed her—and looked bitter and dispossessed, like a man who had had something precious snatched away from him. It wasn't grief; it had nothing to do with grief. Was that why any compassion she felt for him was purely in the abstract? Because he had said "my wife" in the same tone he might have used to refer to his horse, or his car? He had been bereft, she couldn't doubt that, but a part of that had been personal outrage.

The desk telephone rang, and the officer in charge answered it. He listened briefly, his dark gaze on Jenny and then on Mary, before he hung up; it might have been her imagination that made him look disappointed.

"So," he said, contemplating them all, and it was clear that he didn't know quite what to do with them, appetizing though they were. Daniel Brennan had paid his fines. St. Ives had resisted, but without sufficient violence. In that deserted area, the peace hadn't been disturbed. Olfactory evidence to the contrary, Jenny was sober. It was true that a police car had been diverted on what proved to be an unnecessary errand, but that happened all the time.

He fixed his stare on Mary, who sat with her raincoat collar turned up around her throat—but that wasn't remarkable, because from time to time she shivered, although he himself found the room quite warm. "You will wish to press charges?"

It was from her door, out of halfway comprehensible motives and a decision neither weighed nor studied, that a woman in need of help had been turned away. "No," said Mary. "We had an argument, as I told you, but it was all a misunderstanding."

She looked at St. Ives as she spoke, and saw that hatred, like love, was not so easily dispelled. He must have lived with his loathing like a new marriage bond for forty-eight hours, and along came a bony eighteen-year-old from the East, breaking it. Would he have a carry-over, a stubborn belief that she was still somehow involved?

She stood up. "May we go now . . . ?

She assumed that the police would escort the man she had known as Owen St. Ives back to his car, and that he would then turn it over to the place he had rented it from and resume his own blue car and get out of here; she didn't care. She waited with Jenny while Brennan went to get his, aware of an occasional curious glance from the few passers-by at the sight of two Anglo women outside the police station at this hour, not caring about that either.

In the bluish glow, Jenny dragged her hair over her shoulder and studied the ends fiercely. "I did see Brian at the market this afternoon. I lied to you about that."

"I know. I also—" began Mary, and stopped. Why pile pain upon pain? Jenny had saved them both, and been deceived, appallingly in the second case, by two men in a row. She would have quite enough to live with apart from the knowledge that Brian Beardsley had done his best to get her interred in a Mexican prison. Later, if it became necessary—but not now, when Jenny had taken such a physical and mental beating.

Brennan came back with his car, and held the door while Jenny wobbled into the back. He didn't immediately hand Mary in. He said curiously, "Did you mind a great deal, about St. Ives?"

How noticing he was, when he had only observed them together at the police station. And had she minded, apart from that instinctive recoil in the car, as though she had received a lash? The haunting look of Spence—but something had made her back off from Spence at the last minute; not that there was a murderous bone in his body, but he hadn't been for her.

"No," said Mary, and Brennan took her hand contentedly. "You can't go anywhere, because of your car. You'll be here in the morning."

"Yes, I will." Whether it was fatigue or something else, Mary felt suddenly shy with him, as though they were meeting for the first time on this chilly dark alien street. And, in effect, they would be starting all over again. "I haven't even thanked you yet, Daniel." It tasted new on her tongue, and adventurous.

"We have, I hope, all the time in the world," said Brennan.

The man whose real name turned out to be Wesley Hale did not have a carry-over of any kind. At some time before dawn, his northbound car crossed the median and flipped over, killing him instantly. Tragically, said the short newspaper account, he was to have attended the funeral later in the day of his wife, Charlotte, a recent murder victim. (See related story.) As there was no alcohol involved, it was the official surmise that he had fallen asleep at the wheel.

But of course the police had not seen his robbed and furious eyes.

Jenny had had an abrupt longing for her parents, and went home with a gained weight of a pound and a half, which was like a cautious climb up an icy hill. Mary did not send her the clipping.

She did forward an item spotted by Daniel in a financial journal: "The fight for control of Payne-Howard, the nation's second-largest manufacturer of burglar alarms and fire-warning systems, has ended with the confirming of Hiram Aufderheide, 60, as president. Allegations of instability had been brought against Aufderheide, who two weeks ago was incommunicado in Mexi—Please turn to Page 14, Col. 5."